MURDER
in
OKOBOJI

MURDER in OKOBOJI

Peter Davidson

SWEET MEMORIES PUBLISHING

A Division of Sweet Memories, Inc.

sweetmemories@mchsi.com

This book is a work of fiction. Although several real people have cameo roles in the story, all of the main characters are fictitious and any resemblance of these fictitious characters to real persons is purely coincidental. When persons are mentioned by their real names, they are represented in fictitious situations and the reader should not infer that these events or dialogue ac-tually occurred. Some events in the story may be based upon events that actually happened, but the portrayal of these events are the product of the author's imagination and are not intended to represent those events as they may have occurred.

ISBN: 978-0-9762718-2-6
Library of Congress Control Number: 2009902613
First printing July, 2009

Published by Sweet Memories Publishing, Sweet Memories, Inc.,
P.O. Box 497, Arnolds Park, IA 51331-0497.

PRINTED IN THE UNITED STATES OF AMERICA

10 9 8 7 6 5 4 3 2 1

Editor: Beverly Peterson

Graphic Design: Debbie Wilson

Front Cover Photo: Cindy Frederick

Back Cover Photo: David DeVary

Readers: Konnie Bartolo, Stuart Burton, Kristi Matheason, Chris Peterson, Les Peterson, Robin Peterson, Michele Sayre, Jeremy Schendel, Joel Schendel, Kelsey Schendel, Kim Schendel, Nancy Schendel, Neil Schendel, Barb Schomaker, John Smith, Jean Tennant, Dr. Keith Wells

Dedication

This book is dedicated to all who seek to unravel the mysteries of life. To those who realize that things are not always what they seem. To those who know that there are things going on that we suspect but that we cannot prove for certain. To those who would find it interesting, even fascinating, to eavesdrop on the private conversations, deeds, and misdeeds of the rich and powerful. To those to whom one of the great secrets of Okoboji in the past one hundred years will be revealed – about murder in Okoboji.

Peter Davidson

Chapter

1

There are those who claim that I am to blame for what happened – that it is somehow my fault. But I have a clear conscience. After all, all I did was to write a book. It was a novel, *Okoboji*, which is set in the Lake Okoboji resort area of northwest Iowa. Am I to blame for his actions just because he read the book, became intrigued with Okoboji, and came to visit? I think not.

Yet, the task of trying to unravel what happened, to make some sense of it, and to report it seems to have fallen upon my shoulders. I have tried to do so as fairly and accurately as I can, for this is the duty and responsibility of a writer.

Please realize that this was not an easy task, for the true story is known to only a few people. It never made the newspapers, radio, or television. The rich and powerful have a way to make sure that stories like this don't become known to the rank and file. Thus, as you read this account, if you are a local, you are likely to say to yourself, "How could something like this happen, right here under my nose, and I didn't know about it?" Well, I just explained that in the beginning of this paragraph. Please accept this as fact.

As far as my involvement goes, even though he said that my book inspired him to come to Okoboji, I met him only once. We did visit for more than an hour on that occasion and I must admit that I was intrigued and impressed by him. We actually got along quite famously, but ours was only a social discussion about lakes, cars, boats, Rock 'N Roll music, and beer – all the essential stuff for a happy and content life.

I do know all of the others involved in the story – I know them very well. And one of them in particular shared my viewpoint that this story needed to be told. He, or maybe it is a she – I'm not going to offer a hint or clue, since they still live in Okoboji and want to continue doing so - provided me with valuable insight into what happened behind closed doors and who was trying to do what to whom, when, where, and why. Bernstein and Woodward had their Deep Throat in Watergate, and in this story, I had mine.

Yes, the police have talked to me but, if need be, I will plead journalistic immunity to protect the identity of my sources of information.

I should provide a little background information for those of you who aren't familiar with Okoboji, the community, or *Okoboji*, the novel.

The Lake Okoboji resort area, simply referred to as "Okoboji" by the locals and tourists, consists of four small towns, Spirit Lake, Okoboji, Arnolds Park, and Milford, along a ten-mile stretch of Highway 71 in northwest Iowa. The area is a summertime paradise with beautiful lakes, amusement parks, outdoor concerts, great restaurants, and numerous happening bars with live entertainment. Even though there is a town named Okoboji and the name, "Okoboji," is commonly used to describe the entire tourist area, most of the action is in the town of Arnolds Park. There is an amusement park that draws people of all ages, quaint shops, restaurants, the Roof Garden Ballroom, and bars, bars, and more bars.

Okoboji is, in fact, a more popular tourist destination than either the Bridges of Madison County or the Field of Dreams, both of which are also in Iowa and both of which became nationally known because of books and movies. Okoboji is fifteen miles north of Spencer, Iowa where the public library is located that was home to the cat, Dewey, who was the subject of the nationwide number one bestselling book, *Dewey, the Small-Town Library Cat Who Touched the World*.

Okoboji is also the home of the University of Okoboji, which is loved dearly by all who have had the pleasure of attending it, or who have just had a chance to enjoy its magnificently beautiful campus. All Okoboji residents are proud of the fact that the University of Okoboji football team, the Fighting Phantoms, has been unbeaten for over thirty years straight. One of the highlights of the year in Okoboji is Saturday, September 31 when the Fighting Phantoms play the University of Nebraska and Notre Dame football teams in a double header. A double header that the University of Okoboji Fighting Phantoms has never lost.

Okay, the University of Okoboji is a fictitious university that was dreamt up by Herman and Emil Richter and a couple of other locals back in the 1970's. They chose 1878 as the official origination date for the University for a very simple reason – they'd only have to wait a few years for a centennial celebration. The University of Okoboji sponsors numerous annual events such as a bicycle ride around the lake, soccer tournaments, rugby tournaments, and many other activities and has raised hundreds of thousands of dollars for charity. Even though the University is fictitious, shirts, drinking cups, jackets, ashtrays, and numerous other souvenirs bearing the University of Okoboji name and logo can be purchased throughout the Okoboji area.

Every summer, more than a million tourists visit Okoboji. The locals, summertime residents, and tourists consider Okoboji to be a magical place like no other.

A couple of years ago, I wrote a novel that is set in the Lake Okoboji resort area. The novel, *Okoboji*, is the story of a handsome, rich, and famous movie star, Alex Gideon, who becomes disgruntled with his fabulous but flaky life, the demands of his sleazy manager, and the smothering fans, and decides that he needs a break from it all. But where can he go that he isn't recognized? He decides to let fate decide. He places a map of the United States on a dartboard, launches a dart, and vows to take his hiatus wherever the dart lands. Well, the dart lands on Okoboji, in Iowa. Alex decides that Okoboji might just be the perfect getaway – somewhere small, quiet, and quaint where probably no one ever heard of him. Perfect.

Alex disguises himself and takes a circuitous route to Okoboji. He arrives in the middle of July and finds that Okoboji is not the quiet getaway that he had pictured but is, instead, filled with upbeat locals and partying tourists. Alex falls in love with Okoboji, as nearly all who visit her do, becomes involved in the local culture, and falls in love with a fabulous woman who seems to want nothing to do with this stranger from out of town. And, the story continues from there.

Okoboji, the novel, contains dozens of real businesses and around fifty real people who are identified by their real names. I am pleased to say that every one of those people was delighted to be included. Since then, dozens of locals and tourists have asked if I would include them in my next book. I would have been happy to accommodate all of them, but I can only include those names that were actually involved in what happened, which, by the way, is quietly referred to as *The Incident* by those who were involved.

So, there you have it. That's how and why I came to write this account of various deeds and misdeeds that were interwoven and that culminated in murder in Okoboji.

Or, was it? Truth, like beauty, is in the eye of the beholder and ultimately, you will have to decide for yourself whether this story is fact or fiction - whether it was murder or was not.

In the novel, *Okoboji*, I liberally used the names of real people and portrayed them as being good, honorable, and decent, which they are. In this book, however, I have changed the names of the people most deeply involved in *The Incident* since I want to continue living in Okoboji, and I want to continue living, period. You get my drift, I am sure. By that same token, when you recognize someone in the story who is identified by their real name, you can be assured that they are good, honorable, and decent and were not involved in any way in the misdeeds that are described here.

Now, on with the story.

Chapter

2

It was an Okoboji summer day - temps in the eighties, a slight breeze, sailboats on the lake for a tri-state regatta, women in bikinis on the beach and in motorboats, guys chugging cold beer, and summer residents and tourists coming in for the weekend.

He was a handsome man, well tanned, about six foot two, fit, with long premature silver hair combed back nearly covering his ears. It would have been easy to convince yourself, or anyone within earshot that he was a member of the Kennedy clan – you know, John, Bobby, Teddy, and that bunch. He had that same presence about him, that combination of confidence and charm, that compelled men to want to be his friend and that compelled women to, well, want him.

He might have been fifty years old, but he looked forty, or maybe he was forty and looked fifty; with the silver hair it was hard to tell.

It was about four in the afternoon when he walked into

The Gardens, took a seat at the bar and ordered a Glenlivet scotch on the rocks.

The Central Emporium is an Arnolds Park landmark and is a "must see" destination for everyone who comes to Okoboji. The Central Emporium was originally a ballroom that was subsequently used for several other purposes until a young energetic visionary purchased the building and converted it into about twenty retail shops, a restaurant, and a bar. The building has three levels, with the top two levels used for retail shops selling clothing, gift items, books, and the like. The bottom level is a popular bar, The Gardens, with a huge deck overlooking the crystal clear blue waters of West Lake Okoboji. It, too, is a "must see" destination for anyone who enjoys a cocktail or two or who just wants to see and be seen.

He sipped his Glenlivet as he surveyed the early afternoon crowd that was starting to gather. From the sounds coming from some of the tables, however, it appeared that some of them had started to gather several hours ago.

There was a table of four young men with an older man, all of whom had similar facial characteristics – a father and his four sons, probably. They were having a huge time, telling stories, toasting one another, laughing, and telling more stories. The older man rose. "I propose a toast," he said, slurring his words a bit, "to my sons, Stu, Scott, Les, and Chris – and to myself. We may work too little and play too much, we may sing too loud and off key, we may spend more money than we earn, we may drink more than we can hold, and we may not know what the hell is going on, but dammit, we are not boring.'" This was followed by the smashing of beer mugs in a toast as they burst into a rousing drinking song in four-part harmony, all of which were slightly off key.

I want a beer just like the beer that laid out dear old Dad
It was the beer and the only beer that Daddy ever had
Want a good ol' beer with lots of foam
Took ten men to carry Daddy home
Oh, I want a beer just like the beer that laid out dear old Dad

A man and two women at another table were deep in philosophical discussion. They appeared to be holdovers from the hippie era who were still lost in the sixties and who were still debating life rather than participating in it. "If less is more," one said, gazing off into space, "then we've got our share." Deep stuff.

At another table a half dozen raucous women in their twenties were celebrating what appeared to be a bachelor-ette party – a macabre bachelorette party with the bride-to-be wearing a black veil. That observation was clarified, however, when the woman wearing the veil rose and hoisted a shot of tequila in a toast, "Here's to the miserable, low-down, lyin,' cheatin,' skirt-chasin,' snake in the grass who finally got the message that it's over when I dyed my wedding dress black and wore it to the divorce hearing – and here's to my new Mexican restaurant that I'm going to name *Las Alimony*." The shots of tequila were tossed back and you could hear the shouting a mile away.

9

Four guys at another table were discussing the theme of the movie, *The Bucket List,* which said that a person should make a list of things to do before kicking the bucket, and then go about doing them. That led to a discussion about how to properly quit one's job and how to find the money to pursue the bucket list, which led to a discussion of what they would do if they were suddenly fabulously wealthy, which ultimately led to a discussion of their life's fantasies.

"I'd like to rob a bank," said one guy, "through some clever method where I wouldn't even have to buy a gun or personally set foot inside the bank."

"I want to record a song and make a CD," said another, "and I wouldn't let the fact that I can't sing stop me. And then I want them to play the song at my funeral, over and over. And then when they carry me out of the church I want them to parade me around the block a couple of times and march me through a couple of taverns before they plant me. But before I die I'm going to hide little notes all over the house for my wife's next husband – stuff like 'Boo! Get the hell out of my sock drawer.' I'm going to have so much fun I can't wait to die."

"My life's fantasy is pretty simple – I just want to find the son-of-a-bitch who took my lavender shirt and my black and white checkered sport coat about ten years ago," said another. "It wasn't one of you jokers, was it?"

"All you guys' fantasies are rinky-dink," said the final contributor. "I'm going to run for President of the United States, using only an email campaign and news releases emailed to newspapers around the country. My goal is to get enough write-in votes to end up in the top fifty in the general election. What a fabulous story this will be for my grandchildren and great grandchildren and great-great grandchildren to pass down from generation to generation, about how their forefather, me, ran for President of the United States and out of three hundred million people in the country ended up in the top fifty. Can I count on your vote?"

"New in town?" the man across the bar asked.

He set his Glenlivet on the bar and said, "Yes – my first time in Okoboji – actually my first time in the state of Iowa."

"I'm Zach," said the first man as he extended a well-tanned hand to the stranger.

"I'm Gat," he replied.

"Cat?" Zach asked.

"No, Gat, as in Gatlin. My father was a civil war buff and I was named after a rapid firing piece of field artillery used in the civil war."

"The Gatling Gun," Zach said.

"Right," Gat answered with a smile, "but my mother insisted that the "g" be dropped from the end of the name, making it Gatlin, to disguise it a little bit, I suppose. But I answer to either Gat or Gatlin – either way is fine with me."

"What brings you to Okoboji?" Zach asked.

"I'm on a business trip from my home in Rhode Island to Kansas and Colorado and took a detour here to Okoboji for a little 'R & R' before my meetings next week."

"You good at riddles?" Zach asked.

11

"Well, I never thought about it – average I'd guess," Gat answered.

"Here's one for ya," Zach said. "What's black and white and red all over?"

Gat repressed the urge to tell Zach he'd heard this one before. "I don't know," he replied, playing along.

"A newspaper!" Zach said. "Red, spelled r-e-a-d – get it?"

"Mark, we'll have another round," a man wearing a suit and tie said as he approached the bar. He was about six feet tall and wasn't actually fat, but he was thick, with an ass about two axe handles wide. He had an unruly shock of brown hair that went every which way and a mischievous grin revealing a gap between his two front teeth. If Alfred E. Newman from Mad Magazine had about forty more years on him, he'd probably look exactly like this guy.

"I'll have Jennifer bring it over," the bartender replied.

"Hello, Dick Dick," Zach said.

"Zach, good seeing you," he said as he slapped Zach on the back a couple of times. "Who's your friend?" he continued as he motioned at Gat.

"This is Gatlin from Rhode Island, but you can call him Gat if you want - he's on a business trip but stopped off in Okoboji for the weekend," Zach said.

"Dick Dick - my pleasure," he said as he grasped Gat's hand in his and pumped it vigorously. "A lot of people come here for a weekend and end up staying for a lifetime. I'm in the real estate business - Dick Dick Realty. If you'd like to take a look at a lakeshore house or a condo, I'd be pleased to show you around."

"Thanks, but no thanks," Gat said. "As Zach said, I'm just passing through."

"Well, Gatlin, what's your last name?" Dick Dick asked.

"Guthrie – Gatlin Guthrie," he replied.

"Dick Dick, if you guys are waiting for Punky to show up you might have a long wait," Zach said.

"Why's that?"

"He ran with the big dogs last night and I'd bet he's lying by his dish tonight," Zach explained.

"You and who else?"

"Punky, Pedro, and I started at about five o'clock at the Dry Dock, then we went to The Wharf, then Captain's, then Cocktails for some Karaoke, and finally ended up at Ruebin's where we hooked up with Mike and Gaye Dougherty. The rest of us left before midnight but I think Punky closed up the place."

"What in the hell was he celebrating?"

"He was on a mission to hurt himself," Zach replied. "He was drinking some concoction called *Swim A Mile With Roger* that's about twice as potent as wood alcohol. But, he was in a great mood and was having a wonderful time and just got caught up in it, I think. Hey, summertime in Okoboji."

"I can't believe he's going to miss the first clue," Dick Dick said.

"He made me promise about ten times last night that if

he missed it I would call him with it by 9:15 – nobody ever gets it after the first clue anyway," Zach said.

"That makes sense, I guess," Dick Dick said wistfully. "Well, come join us," he said, motioning to Zach and Gat, as he pointed to a table in the corner occupied by two men.

"I've got to go," Zach said, "but thanks – maybe next time."

"Well, then, Gatlin, don't sit here by yourself, come on over and have a drink with us, and Mark," he said, talking to the bartender, "have Jennifer bring Gatlin another of what he's drinking."

"Can I ask you something?" Gat asked as they walked toward the table.

"Dick Dick, right"?

"Right – why do you repeat your name twice?"

"My dad's name was Herbert Dick and he was a crackerjack salesman. He thought the greatest profession in the world – life's highest calling – was to be a salesman. When I was born he wanted me to have a unique name so if I went into sales it would stick out, that it would be memorable. So, he named me Dick Dick. Dick is both my first name and my last name. I like it. Once people hear my name they never forget it – or me. Like I said, my dad was a crackerjack salesman – he knew all the angles."

"Clever," Gat said.

"Just about everybody calls me Dick Dick and once in a while they call me some other names. I won't get into that, but you can use your imagination," Dick Dick said with a toothy grin.

Gat followed Dick Dick to a table in the corner where one man was aimlessly shuffling a deck of cards and another was draining his cocktail glass. They were a mismatched pair. The one shuffling cards was homely. Just plain homely. He had a long expressionless face and when he looked up at Gat and Dick Dick, his left eye remained half closed. He wore expensive clothes but everything hung on him like the proverbial undertaker whose clothes don't match and never quite fit right. The other man was the image of suave and debonair. He was tanned and fit with long flowing silver hair that matched Gat's. His green golf shirt, tan slacks, and Italian leathers on his feet were also expensive, but he could have worn clothes from a garage sale and he would have looked like a model in a Saks Fifth Avenue catalog.

"Fellas, this is Gatlin Guthrie from Rhode Island," Dick Dick began. "And this is Stephen Southworth the Third," he said pointing to the guy with the droopy eye, "but everybody calls him Sleepy. And this is Lenny Rosenthal," he said gesturing toward the suave one.

"By the way, guys," Dick Dick said, "Zach said that Punky partied hard last night and he probably won't be coming, so let's put the cards away and talk to our new friend here, Gatlin."

"What brings you to Okoboji?" Lenny asked.

"It's kind of a strange story in a way," Gat began, "but a friend of a friend of mine from Rhode Island attended his nephew's wedding to a young woman here in Okoboji a year ago or so."

"That would be Shelly Harken," Dick Dick exclaimed. "She married a guy from Rhode Island last summer. In fact, I was at the wedding – all three of us at this table were there."

"Well," Gat continued, "there were about forty guests from Rhode Island and other parts of the east coast who had never been to Iowa, so the bride's mother . . ."

"That would be Betty Harken," Lenny interrupted.

"The bride's mother," Gat continued, "put together a gift package for each of the east coast guests that consisted of various products from Iowa. There was . . ."

"Sioux Bee Honey, Cookie's Barbeque Sauce, Jolly Time Popcorn, Amana Sausage and all sorts of things," Dick Dick said. "I saw one of the gift packages; I wish they'd have given me one."

"And there was also a copy of a novel set in Okoboji in each of the gift packages," Gat said.

"The book was named *Okoboji*," Lenny said. "We all read it."

"Well," Gat continued, "my friend's friend who attended the wedding fell in love with Okoboji, the area, and also *Okoboji*, the book. He raved so much about his trip to Okoboji that my friend borrowed the book and after he read it he loaned it to me and I read it. So, since I was heading in this general direction anyway – I'm on my way to Kansas and Colorado on business – I added a couple of days to my trip to see Okoboji for myself. And, here I am."

"That's a great story," Sleepy said slowly, dryly. Not only

16

was his eye sleepy, but his voice was too.

"And while I'm here, I'm going to see as many sites described in the book and meet as many people who were in the story as I can," Gat said. "I've already been to the Three Sons clothing store and have met Herman and Emil – Golly Gee," he said, imitating Herman's favorite phrase. "What great guys. And, I'm staying at the Four Seasons Motel, where the character in the book, Alex, stayed and I met Mayor Mike and First Lady Jill who run the place. And, I had a cup of coffee and a scotcheroo at Arnolds Perk."

"That's really great. I live here and I haven't done half that stuff," Lenny said. "So what else is on your agenda to see or do in Okoboji?"

"I understand there's a concert at the Roof Garden Ballroom tonight, so I'm going to stop in for a song or two," Gat said.

"That's the 'Rock the Roof' concert – it's free every Thursday night all summer long – draws a thousand people or more," Dick Dick said. "And what else is on your schedule?"

"I've already walked through some of the shops in the Emporium and I'm going to check out Maestro Horsman at Ruebins and I'd like to take a look at some cars at Lyin' Louie's Lemon Lot."

"Well, Gatlin, my new friend, most of the stuff in the book was true, but the author made up a few things. Even though a few of our car dealers in the area might resemble it, there is no Lyin' Louie's Lemon Lot car dealership – he made that up," Lenny said.

"Anything else I should know about so I don't waste my time chasing after things that don't exist?" Gat asked.

"No, No, I don't think so," Dick Dick answered. "Oh, one thing you'll want to see for sure is the University of Okoboji campus – it's beautiful. It's about four blocks straight east of here."

Lenny and Sleepy nodded their heads in agreement. "Straight east," Sleepy added.

"That's something you'll want to see for sure," Lenny said.

Gat looked at the three of them sitting there somber faced and broke into a grin. "Remember fellas, I read the book, and I know about the University of Okoboji – nice try."

The three broke into laughter. "You can't blame us for trying," Dick Dick said. "Every year we send about a dozen tourists on a wild goose chase looking for the University. One year we even handed out maps. Just some small town guys trying to have a little fun."

"You good at riddles?" Sleepy asked.

"Probably about average," Gat answered.

"Here's one – what's the difference between a wife and a girlfriend?" Dick Dick asked.

"I don't know," Gat answered.

"Forty pounds!" Lenny answered.

"What's the difference between a husband and a boyfriend?" Dick Dick asked.

"Again, I don't know," Gat answered.

"Forty minutes!" Sleepy answered as the three of them howled at the response.

"You know," Gat started, "this is the second time in about a half hour I've been asked if I'm good at riddles. What's up?"

"The Great Okoboji Treasure Hunt," Dick Dick answered. "Every week for ten consecutive weeks the Chamber of Commerce is sponsoring a treasure hunt with a $1,000 weekly prize. Then on the final week, on Labor Day weekend, there's a $5,000 prize."

"Each week they hide a certificate for the money somewhere in the community and then they give a series of clues to its location in the form of a riddle," Lenny said.

"And if you can solve the riddle and find the certificate, the money's yours," Sleepy added.

"There are five clues that are given starting with the first one tonight at nine o'clock after the Rock the Roof concert at the Roof Garden Ballroom. The second clue is given at six o'clock Friday evening, the third clue is at 10 a.m. Saturday, the fourth clue is at 3 p.m. Saturday and the final clue is given Sunday noon," Dick Dick said.

"Some people try to figure out the riddles by themselves and others have formed teams and have given themselves names like 'Einstein's Formulators,' and 'The Riddle Busters,' and stuff like that. The three of us are 'The Three Wise Men,'" Lenny said.

"And your friend, Funky, the guy that got drunk last night – is he part of your group?" Gat asked.

19

"Punky, with a P," Dick Dick said. "Punky's on his own. He fancies himself as being smarter than the three of us put together, but it's hard to tell 'cause none of us have claimed one of the treasures so far."

"It's not about the money for most people," Lenny explained. "It's the challenge."

"And the bragging rights," Sleepy added.

"Has anybody solved a riddle from the first clue?" Gat asked.

"No," Lenny answered, "the quickest anybody's solved a riddle was after the third clue, and that was some grade school kid."

"It was humiliating for The Three Wise Men to get beat by a grade-schooler," Sleepy said.

"The first three clues are usually pretty vague and they usually don't make much sense until after the fourth or fifth clues are given, and then you kick yourself for not figuring it out sooner," Lenny said.

"The third week, we almost won," Dick Dick said. "We figured it out after the fourth clue and got there about fifteen seconds after some goofy-looking guy found the certificate."

"Does the Chamber do this every summer?" Gat asked.

"No, this is the first year," Dick Dick answered. "The tourist traffic has been a little slow here the past couple of summers because of the economy and gas prices. The Chamber came up with the treasure hunt idea to create some excitement, to draw people to the lakes earlier, and to keep them here for the entire weekend."

"Has it worked?" Gat asked.

"It's been wildly successful," Lenny answered. "Tourist traffic is up around thirty percent over the past two summers."

"The only downside is that some of the treasure hunters get a little overly zealous," Dick Dick said. "On the second week, a couple dozen people somehow got the idea that the treasure was buried in the Arnolds Park Cemetery and they headed there with picks and shovels. Fortunately, the police got there just in time before they started digging up bodies. After that, the Chamber announced places where the treasure would not be – such as not underground or not under water – stuff like that."

"Here's one of the riddles," Sleepy said, pulling a sheet of paper from his shirt pocket. "This was from week three.

Clue Number One:

> I may or may not be the best,
> But I think I am the largest.
> You probably cast a glance my way,
> As you whizzed past me the other day.

Clue Number Two:

> From time to time you probably heard my name,
> But didn't know where I was until along I came.
> East, west, north, and south,
> Three of these will help you out.

Clue Number Three:

> A little off the beaten road,
> In a circle around you'll go.
> It doesn't have to be that way,
> Stop, get out, take a walk north I say.

Clue Number Four:

> Slow down,
> When you come into town.
> Even though this is all for fun,
> Don't laugh 'cause my bottom weighs many a ton.

Clue Number Five:

> Paul Simon was loved like this,
> Talkin' about my bottom, that is.
> There's 70 or 80 of me,
> How many clues do you need?"

"Do you know where it is?" Dick Dick asked anxiously.

"Not a clue," Gat replied. "I'm new in town. I don't understand any of the clues."

"It's easier than you think, now that you see all of the clues together," Lenny said. "In fact, you have already gone past the location at least twice since you got here."

"So, where is it?" Gat asked.

"Can't tell you," Dick Dick said. "That would spoil all the fun for you. But, think about it a little bit, and keep your eyes open as you explore Okoboji - you'll figure it out."

"And the new riddle starts tonight after the Rock the Roof concert?" Gat asked.

"Right, make sure you stick around for the reading of the clue," Lenny said. "When the concert starts at six o'clock, the Roof Garden probably will be half full, by seven it will be full, and by the time the concert's over and they have the reading of the clue at nine, it will be overflowing and the sidewalk and street outside the Roof Garden will be packed."

"Just a bunch of small town folks trying to have a little fun," Dick Dick said.

"Gatlin, what do you do for a living?" Lenny asked, changing the topic.

"Oh, I'm self-employed," Gat said.

"Self-employed at what?" Dick Dick asked.

"Well," Gat said slowly, "I guess you'd call me a developer."

"Real estate developments?" Dick Dick asked, sensing that maybe he had stumbled upon a live one.

"No, not really – actually not at all," Gat replied. "I usually need to acquire land for my projects but I'm not a commercial developer. And what do you guys do?" he asked, pointing to Sleepy and Lenny, shifting the conversation away from himself.

They ignored him and pressed on.

"So what kind of projects do you do?" Dick Dick asked.

"Oh, various kinds," Gat replied. "It varies."

"Like what?" Sleepy asked.

Their curiosity was starting to eat at them but Gat continued to be evasive, not wanting to tell them any more than he had to without being rude.

"Well, it just varies," Gat said, "and some of it's kind of sensitive – I'm not really supposed to talk about it. I mean there are other entities involved and we don't want to make an announcement until we have everything buttoned down."

"But I'll bet you're going to Kansas and Colorado to look at possible sites for your project – am I right?" Dick Dick asked with a knowing smile tugging at his lips.

Gat smiled back at him and hesitated for a moment to choose his words.

"I knew it! I just knew it!" Dick Dick exclaimed before Gat could get a word out.

"Something like that, but I really can't talk about it, guys. Got to button things down, you know," Gat said.

"We understand," Lenny said. "We're all businessmen of one kind or another and we're just curious – didn't mean to pry."

"Thanks for being understanding. Maybe if I come back through here in a year or two we can have a drink or two together and I can tell you all about it," Gat said.

"Great, sounds great," Sleepy said. "We'll look forward to it."

Gat checked his watch. "The Rock the Roof concert started about a half hour ago so I'd better get going or I'll miss it. Maybe I'll see you guys around over the weekend."

"When are you leaving?" Dick Dick asked.

"Probably Monday; maybe Tuesday, depending on how much fun I'm having here in Okoboji."

Gat shook hands all around the table, extended a few pleasantries, and headed for the Roof Garden Ballroom. As he climbed the stairs they were singing that song again, with gusto, and the bachelorettes had joined in. Didn't sound too bad – not bad at all.

I want a beer just like the beer that laid out dear old Dad
It was the beer and the only beer that Daddy ever had
Want a good ol' beer with lots of foam ...

Chapter

3

The three of them sat at the table silently until it appeared that Gatlin was out of earshot.

"Are you thinkin' what I'm thinkin'?" Dick Dick asked.

"He's into something big," Sleepy said.

"And he's damn evasive about it," Lenny said. "He's two thousand miles from home and there's no reason for him to be so damn secretive about it unless it's something big – really big."

"Did you see his watch?" Dick Dick asked. "It's a Patek Philippe Calendario – costs about forty grand. And his diamond ring – a full carat, colorless grade E or F – maybe even D, with a fluorescence rating of none to negligible. High quality; high, high quality."

"What makes you think you know so much about diamonds?" Sleepy asked.

"Hell," Dick Dick said, "I've been married three times – two wives I couldn't keep and one I couldn't get rid of. I've bought a lot of diamonds in my day. I know diamonds."

"That proves it, then. He's a high roller and he's into something big," Lenny said.

"And we need to find out what it is," Dick Dick said.

The three of them jumped up in unison and charged the bar. "Dixie, Dixie," Dick Dick said to the tall woman sitting at the bar talking to a young woman in her twenties, "can we go to your office and use your computer for a couple of minutes?"

She shrugged. "Sure, Dick Dick," she said as she handed over a set of keys. "It's the silver one."

The three of them charged up the stairs leaving The Gardens in their wake.

❖　❖　❖

The two of them sat silently, as they had for the past half hour, until the three buffoons were out of earshot.

"It's *Him*. I know it's *Him*." the blonde said.

"I couldn't hear everything they said," the redhead replied, "but he's got an east coast accent and they were talking about some big deal he's got cooking."

"And he looks the part," the blonde said.

"It's *Him*. I can feel it in my heart; it's *Him*." the redhead said.

"And he's on his way to the Roof Garden," the blonde said.

"Let's go," the redhead said. And they were off.

❖　❖　❖

The Three Wise men rushed toward the far end of the hallway on the second floor of the Central Emporium. To the left of the stairs leading to the top floor was a door that Dick Dick frantically tried to unlock. He wiggled the silver key back and forth and finally the handle turned.

They entered the room cautiously and fumbled around for a light switch. Finally, Sleepy found it and flicked it on. It was a small room under the stairs, slightly larger than a storage closet found under the stairs of a typical home. The ceiling was slanted at the same angle as the stairs above it and boxes were piled high against the only square wall in the room. There was an old metal desk with a straight back chair behind it, but the only thing that mattered to The Three Wise Men was sitting on top of the desk, turned on and ready for use. Dick Dick plopped down on the chair and logged onto the computer.

"He should be easy to find," Lenny said. "Rhode Island's a small state."

Dick Dick entered "Gatlin Guthrie, Rhode Island," in Google and hit search. Instantly, the name Gatlin Guthrie was splashed all over the monitor.

Dick Dick clicked on "Gatlin Guthrie, Entrepreneur," and the three of them gasped in unison.

Lenny read aloud, "Gatlin Guthrie, grandson of former Rhode Island Governor, Bart Guthrie, is following in his family's entrepreneurial spirit as he scores big with one huge government contract after another after another. His latest venture, a contract with the U.S. Government Defense Department is sure to add to his rapidly growing reputation as one of the most knowledgeable and savvy government contract power brokers in America. The project, estimated to be in the range of seven or eight hundred million dollars . . . ."

"Ho-ly shit," Dick Dick said. "We mess around with projects worth a few hundred thousand – maybe even a million or two once in a while, but this is the b-i-g time.

"Boys, this is too good of an opportunity to let slip away." Dick Dick continued. "If he's going to put his new plant or factory, or whatever it is, in Kansas or Colorado, he could just as well put it in Okoboji."

"So, how are we going to get a piece of the action?" Sleepy asked.

"First we need to find out what he's up to," Dick Dick said. "But I do know one thing, there isn't a development in the world that doesn't start with the land – a big piece of land, maybe a square mile or maybe even more."

"I think I know where you're going with that," Lenny said. "Punky."

"Right," Dick Dick said. "Punky still has that section and half section three miles west of the lake. The idiot always said it would make a great industrial site, maybe it's going to turn out he was right."

"How much is it worth?" Sleepy asked.

"It's clay and light, sandy soil – fair farm land at best. As farm land it's worth maybe three thousand an acre."

"And as an industrial site?" Sleepy asked.

"Depends on how badly the developer wants it, mainly," Dick Dick said. "In cities, land sometimes sells for ten or twenty million dollars an acre for a development, but land out here would never sell for anything like that, there's too much of it."

"So what's Punky's land worth as a development?" Lenny asked.

"It probably doesn't matter so much what it's worth as what Punky wants for it," Dick Dick said. "I've tried to get him to list it for sale for years but he's convinced it's the greatest industrial site in North America and that it's worth over $10,000 an acre. So I never listed it for sale 'cause I knew I could never sell it for that price. Why waste my time?"

"Let's put our cards on the table, and let's be honest about our dishonest intentions," Lenny said. "We're talking about trying to buy Punky's land cheap and then quickly turning around and selling it to Gatlin at a big profit, right?"

"Paying ten thousand an acre isn't cheap," Sleepy said.

"It's like the stock market or like buying gold – it doesn't matter what you pay if you can sell it to the next guy for more," Dick Dick explained. "And keep in mind, if Gatlin's got a government contract, they probably budgeted a dollar amount for the land and the bureaucratic idiots probably based it on the value of land in Manhattan or in Washington, D.C. I see an opportunity here. It's worth a shot."

"But Punky's sister owns half, right?" Lenny asked.

"Right," Dick Dick replied.

"Didn't you date her back in the old days?" Lenny asked.

31

"For a little while; we were kids." Dick Dick said.

"Well, is she more reasonable than Punky on the price of that land?" Lenny asked.

"I don't know," Dick Dick replied curtly.

"Well, you know her," Lenny said. "Could you talk to her and find out?"

"That was a long time ago, she might not even remember me," Dick Dick said.

"What he's trying to say is that it ended poorly. Ain't that right, Dick Dick?" Sleepy said more as a statement of fact than as a question.

Dick Dick nodded his head in agreement. "It ended poorly."

"Good goin'," Lenny said sarcastically.

"Molly. Her name's Molly." Sleepy said.

"Right," Dick Dick agreed.

"Where does she live now?" Lenny asked.

"Down south somewhere – Gulfport or somewhere like that," Dick Dick said.

"It's Gulf Shores, Alabama," Sleepy said. "Punky talks about her once in a while when you're not around, Dick Dick. She's an artist – makes new stuff out of old stuff and if you can guess what it used to be you get a discount."

"She sounds like a nut case like Punky," Lenny said.

"I saw her a couple of years ago when she came to visit Punky," Sleepy said. "She's cool. She's smart and pretty and funny. But her one flaw is that she thinks Punky is a genius. I think she'd do whatever he says on selling that land."

"Well, the hell with Punky," Lenny said. "Is there any other piece of land around here that we could get our hands on?"

"Not that I know of, not of enough acres all in one piece," Dick Dick replied. "If the price was right I could probably put a few adjoining pieces together, but that would take time – maybe months. If we want to get in on what Gatlin's got going, I don't think time's on our side."

"So, what's our next step?" Sleepy asked.

"Well, just in case there's something here that we can get in on, there are two things that we need to do," Dick Dick said. "First, we need to keep Punky away from Gatlin or he'll just sell his land directly to Gatlin and cut us out. Second, we need to find out what Gatlin's up to, if anything, that we can get involved in."

"Count me in," Lenny said. "So, what's next?"

"I need to think this out," Dick Dick said. "Let's meet at Maxwell's in about an hour."

"Going for a boat ride?" Sleepy asked.

"Yup. I always do my best thinking out on the water." Dick Dick said. "See you at Maxwell's."

Chapter
4

Gat had no trouble finding the Roof Garden Ballroom; he just followed his ears. He could hear the strains of Elvis Presley's "Burning Love" from three blocks away.

The Roof Garden is a shell of a building with a cement floor that is on the east edge of the grounds of Historic Arnolds Park Amusement Park. It is the oldest amusement park west of the Mississippi River and is the home of one of the few remaining original wooden roller coasters in America. The amusement park is somewhat of a throwback to an earlier, simpler era with rides such as the Tilt-A-Whirl, Log Flume, Ferris Wheel, Merry-Go-Round, and Bumper Cars. It is void of the high tech, glitzy rides that are found at some of its more modern contemporaries. Arnolds Park Amusement Park is simply a charming place where an entire family can have a good time.

The street outside the Roof Garden was lined with vintage cars, to set the mood for the classic Rock 'N Roll music being played inside. Gatlin strolled by the cars before going inside - a sparkling black '58 Chevy Impala, a '56 Nomad, a '57 Chevy convertible, a '57 Ford Skyliner, a customized '58 Mercury, a '59 Cadillac convertible, and a '54 Corvette – all in mint condition.

Gatlin stepped inside the double doors to the Roof Garden and surveyed the scene. To the left, in the front of the building, was a large stage with a half dozen musicians cranking out Sam The Sham's "Wooly Bully." A sign hanging on the wall behind the band identified them as *Rev. Isiah Brown's Helluva Band.*

Just inside the door along the wall to the left were three long tables filled with record albums, CD's, shirts emblazoned with the slogan, *Iowa Rocks,* and other music related memorabilia.

In the back of the building was the bar with people standing in line ten deep to purchase a cool beverage to combat the heat, or, simply, to party.

There were rows of chairs that were filled with maybe seven or eight hundred people and several hundred more milled around the back of the ballroom or stood along the sides to get a better view of the band.

"Welcome to Rock the Roof; your first time here?" a woman asked.

"First time in Okoboji – actually, first time in Iowa," Gat answered.

"Let me give you a little background then," she said. "The Rock the Roof concerts are presented free every Thursday night in the summer. They're sponsored by the Iowa

Rock 'N Roll Museum, which is part of the Iowa Rock 'N Roll Music Association. I'm Doris, the Executive Director. Welcome."

"Thank you, I'm Gatlin Guthrie from Rhode Island," he replied. "I'm passing through on a business trip and am just checking out the sites."

"You probably don't know anyone in Okoboji, then," Doris said.

"I met a few people but I don't see anyone here that I recognize," Gat replied.

"Then let me introduce you to some people who can help get you acquainted," Doris said as she motioned for two couples to join them.

"This is Gatlin from Rhode Island and this is Bob and Barb and Dave and Bev, and I've got to go," Doris said as she turned and headed back to the merchandise tables.

"Can I buy you a drink?" Bob asked.

"I'd have a cola," Gatlin replied.

Bob and Dave headed toward the bar while Barb and Bev engaged Gat in conversation.

"Bob reminds me of someone – he looks like . . . "

"The singer, B.J. Thomas," Barb interrupted.

"No, no – not at all. I was going to say he resembles Patrick Swayze, the actor," Gat said.

"Thank you, Thank you," Barb and Bev said in unison.

"A couple of years ago Dave started telling Bob that he looked exactly like B.J. Thomas and Bob started believing it and started dressing like B.J. and wearing his hair like B.J.

and now he's taking singing lessons – he's driving us all nuts," Barb said, as Bev nodded her head in agreement.

"He's the guy who was referred to as B.J. Thomas in the *Okoboji* novel," Gat said with a smile.

"It was like throwing gasoline on a bonfire," Bev said with a smile.

"Actually, we've had a lot of fun with it," Barb said, "but I wish he'd just go back to being Bob, or even Patrick Swayze."

Bob and Dave returned with the drinks and passed them out.

"Gatlin was telling us that he thinks you look like someone famous," Barb said. "Tell him Gatlin."

"Well, I think you're a dead ringer for, uh, John Cougar Mellencamp," Gat said.

"Who?" they all said.

"Or maybe Patrick Swayze," Gat said.

Bob got a wide smile on his face as he looked back and forth between Gat and the two women. "They put you up to this, right?"

"No, not at all," Gat said. "Who do you think you look like?"

"I always thought I looked a little bit like Patrick Swayze before these guys tried to convince me I look like B.J. Thomas," Bob replied.

"Can you sing?" Gat asked.

Bob hesitated for a moment and finally smiled and said, "I can sing loud."

"Can you sing good?" Gat asked.

"Maybe not as good as the real B.J.," Bob conceded.

"Well, there you have it," Gat said. "Patrick Swayze."

Gat bought a round of drinks and excused himself so he could wander through the crowd. It was an older crowd, maybe from forty on up – just what you'd expect for a concert of classic Rock 'N Roll oldies. He felt like he fit right in.

They discretely followed Gat from a distance of maybe fifteen feet, watching his every move, never letting his eyes meet theirs. "Look at the way he studies every person and every object in the room, just like a real professional," the blonde said.

"It's got to be *Him.*" the redhead said. "Who else would be so observant, capturing every minute detail."

"It's *Him.* alright," the blonde agreed. "Now we need to follow our plan and not be too obvious but still be obvious enough to attract his attention . . . ."

"When the time is right, we'll strike," the redhead added.

Gat wandered through the crowd, which had swelled to a packed house just like Dick Dick, Sleepy, and Lenny had predicted, and there was still more than an hour before the reading of "The Clue" for the new Treasure Hunt.

It was a hot summer evening and the combination of over a thousand warm bodies, no air conditioning, and no circulation in the building led to a very stuffy, muggy atmosphere. Gat squeezed his way through the crowd toward the exit and joined hundreds of others who had gathered outside.

He strolled along the sidewalk toward the lake, leisurely enjoying the glorious sunshine and slight breeze.

Gat admired the bronze statue of Captain Steve Kennedy and two children on the pier along the lake and read the plaque describing the fantastic contributions that Captain Steve had made to the Maritime Museum, the amusement park, and to all of Okoboji.

Sitting at a table in the outside patio of Maxwell's Restaurant, just south of the pier, were The Three Wise Men, huddled in serious discussion. Perhaps they were trying to make a list of possible locations where the next treasure would be hid so they could get a jump on the competition. Perhaps they were planning their next big Okoboji business deal. Gat's first impulse was to walk across the cul-de-sac separating the pier and Maxwell's and buy The Three Wise Men a drink, but he decided it would be best not to interrupt them and break their train of thought.

Next to the pier on a wide dock that extended a hundred feet out into the lake was a bar, identified as "Pirate Jack's." Gat made his way to the bar and ordered a cola.

"I don't think we've met," the guy behind the bar said in a husky voice as he extended a hand. "I'm Jack."

"Pirate Jack?" Gat asked as they shook hands.

"One and the same," he said.

"I'm Gatlin from Rhode Island," Gat said. "Just passing through and enjoying the beautiful area. This is a great little bar you've got here."

"I just run it about four months in the summer during

the tourist season, but it put my kids through college," Jack said.

"I've got a riddle for you," he continued. "What goes up but never goes down?"

"You got me, I don't know," Gat answered.

"Your age!" Jack replied as he turned to wait on a blonde and a redhead who approached the bar.

Gat finished his cola and slowly walked back toward the Ballroom. People were wandering around the pier, the sidewalk, and the retail shops across from the Roof Garden, apparently waiting until it was time to move in closer for the announcement of The Clue.

Gat squeezed himself inside the door of the Roof Garden. It was futile to try to work his way closer to the stage since people were now standing shoulder to shoulder along the sides of the ballroom all the way up to the stage and there were maybe two or three hundred people standing in front of the stage on what was intended to be a dance floor.

The poster on the wall identified the second performer of the evening as *Okoboji's Own Damon Dotson*. Dotson and his five-piece band played both cover songs and original songs from Dotson's latest CD. They finished the evening's concert with an upbeat original song, "Good Night," that was one of the best songs of the evening.

Gat checked his watch; it was 8:55 – almost time for the reading of The Clue. Even though he didn't know enough about the community to be a worthy competitor in the treasure hunt, he had to admit to himself that he was curious and he was actually anxious to hear what the clue was.

Outside the building, a police car slowly made its way down the street toward the pier with its lights flashing. It made a U-Turn in the cul-de-sac at the end of the street and pulled up in front of the Roof Garden. Two armed police officers in uniform, a man and a woman, got out of the police car, unlocked the trunk, and removed a metal strongbox. They each grabbed a handle of the box and carried it into the Roof Garden. Even though the place was packed shoulder to shoulder, the crowd made a pathway for the officers, who carried the strongbox to the stage. The atmosphere was electric with anticipation.

The police officers placed the strongbox on a table on the stage and each stood at attention on opposite sides of the table.

A handsome man with salt and pepper hair wearing shorts and an *Iowa Rocks* T-shirt approached the microphone. The buzz in the crowd died immediately.

"I'm Tom Golden, president of the Iowa Rock 'N Roll Music Association," he said. "We hope you enjoyed tonight's Rock the Roof concert." Wildly enthusiastic applause erupted and died just as abruptly as Tom again approached the microphone.

"It is my pleasure to introduce the honorable mayor of Arnolds Park, Mayor Mike Mitchell," Golden said and again the place erupted in enthusiastic applause, which stopped suddenly as Mayor Mitchell took the microphone.

Mayor Mitchell reached into his pocket and retrieved

a large key that he held high above his head for everyone to see. "This is the key to the box that holds the first clue to this week's Great Okoboji Treasure Hunt," he said. The applause was deafening.

Mayor Mitchell handed the key to Golden and he approached the box. The crowd waited in silent anticipation. But try as he might, Golden couldn't seem to get the key to work. Maybe the lock was broken. Maybe it was the wrong key, or the wrong lock. He fumbled with it again and again, but no luck.

Golden approached the microphone and the crowd hung on his every word. "Has anyone got a . . ." he paused for effect. ". . . a sledgehammer?" he asked.

The crowd moaned; they groaned. And then Golden turned, walked to the locked box, slipped the key in the lock, whipped open the box, and grabbed an envelope, which he handed to Mayor Mitchell. The crowd waited in rapt attention.

Gat loved a good show and he loved showmanship and these Okoboji guys were playing it to the hilt.

Mayor Mitchell opened the envelope and read slowly, "The first clue for this week's Great Okoboji Treasure Hunt is as follows:

'Sometimes our best plans fall,
Because we simply think too small.
And that could be true of me,
Me in all of my majesty.' "

Notepads and pens appeared from pockets and purses everywhere as people scribbled down the clue. Mayor Mitchell read it one more time, and the race was on.

People filed out of the Roof Garden mumbling to themselves or talking to their riddle-solving team members, analyzing every word, every phrase. Most looked resigned to the fact, though, that they wouldn't be solving anything from the first clue; they'd have to wait until tomorrow.

"He didn't write down a word of the clue, so he's not here for the treasure hunt," the redhead said.

"But he soaked it all in like a sponge," the blonde said. "It's *Him*."

Gat stood off to the side of the door until most of the crowd had filed out. Finally, when it was safe, he made his way to the merchandise table.

"Well, Gatlin," Doris said, "how did you like our concert?"

"Loved it. Both bands were great and I especially enjoyed several of Dotson's original songs," Gat said.

"Everyone, your attention please," Doris said, addressing the work force behind the merchandise tables, "this is Gatlin from Rhode Island. It's his first time in Okoboji and his first Rock the Roof concert – and, Gatlin, this is Jackie, Wanda, Paul, Karen, Naomi, Brad, Louise, Carol, Becky and Barb – all volunteers at the Museum."

Gat purchased a Damon Dotson CD and a blue T-shirt with "Iowa Rocks" on the front. He chatted briefly with the museum volunteers and headed for the exit.

He checked his watch; it was 9:35 – the shank of the evening and perfect timing for catching a song or two from Maestro Horsman at Ruebin's bar.

He walked leisurely toward the pier and stopped for a moment to watch the boats slowly motor by, creating gentle waves that slapped against the concrete wall of the pier.

The Three Wise Men were still in animated conversation on Maxwell's patio and again Gat decided to leave them alone. After all, he had only shared a cocktail and an hour's conversation with them. They probably would have no interest in becoming better acquainted since he'd be leaving town in a couple of days anyway and would most likely never see them again.

Gat followed the sidewalk along the lake, past Bob's Drive-In and up the slight incline towards downtown Arnolds Park where the bars were starting to rock.

It was the perfect pace for the blonde and the redhead to keep up from some fifty feet behind him without breaking a sweat and without attracting attention.

"That settles it, then," Dick Dick said to Sleepy and Lenny. "We've got our game plan. We've each got our jobs to do and we'll put the plan in action tomorrow morning. If it works like I think it could, we will make millions by this time next week and if we've guessed wrong on what our new friend Gatlin is up to, no harm done."

"A win-win, no-lose situation," Lenny said.

"Amen," Sleepy agreed.

Chapter
5

Downtown Arnolds Park, Broadway Street, was rock-in'. It appeared that a good share of the Rock the Roof crowd had not gone home after the concert and the reading of The Clue, but that they had simply moved the party downtown. Add another thousand partiers in their twenties and you've got the scene.

Music wafting from a half dozen clubs filled the air and hundreds of party goers mingled on the sidewalks or stood in line to pay a $20 cover charge for the privilege of paying $5 for a beer and getting their ribs cracked as they squeezed their way through the crowd. But, if you're in your twenties it's worth it because you never know, this could be your lucky night. And if you're past your twenties, just getting squeezed might make it worth it.

The bars were all at full capacity, and then some, and there were forty or fifty people waiting in line at each of the clubs until someone left so they could get in. Gat surveyed the situation at Ruebins and was about to leave when a voice behind him said, "Gat, follow me." It was Zach.

Zach led Gat past Captain's Getaway, around the corner and into the alley at the back. "You'd stand in line a half hour or an hour to get in; this is the back way into Ruebins, known only by the locals."

The alley was dark as coal and there were empty beer cases stacked along one side, plastic bags filled with garbage piled high, a dumpster or two, and several other unidentifiable objects along the way. Every couple of steps there was a new, foul, odor like nothing Gat had ever smelled in his life. The footing was uneven and it seemed that every time Gat put his left foot down he stepped in a rut and every time he put his right foot down he stepped on something that resembled a body. Small red lights glowed off in the distance.

"See those red lights, that's smokers," Zach said. "Since the state banned smoking in bars, the locals sneak out the back door and smoke out here and then they re-enter through the back door without having to stand in line to get in the front door."

Zach and Gat finally reached the back door of Ruebins, which was propped open for ventilation. As they entered, several high-pitched screams could be heard coming from the alley behind them.

"Girls," Zach said. "That alley is no place for girls. Hear them screaming – the dark has something to do with it, and the dumpsters and the smell and the mysterious red lights, but what really gets them is that the ground is so uneven they think they're walking on bodies. Ain't that a hoot!"

"Ya, a real hoot," Gat agreed.

Ruebins was just as Gat had pictured it – long and narrow with the bar off to the left as he stood facing the front. The "back door" was actually a side door, since there was about as much of the room to the right of the door as there was to the left. Instruments, suitcases, and gadgets and gizmos of all kinds hung from the ceiling. And there it was on the wall above the bar – a moose head with the slogan, "A saloon without a moose is just a bar."

In the front, just inside the front door, was the stage where Maestro Horsman performed his musical magic. He was in the middle of "I Don't Want To Go Home," by Southside Johnny and the Asbury Jukes. Southside Johnny was one of the more popular acts from New Jersey and was widely known up and down the east coast. Even though Southside Johnny was equally as talented as some of the other New Jersey artists that became international stars like Springsteen and Bon Jovi, Southside Johnny and the Asbury Jukes were hardly known west of the Hudson River. It surprised and pleased Gat to hear some Southside Johnny, and to hear such a rousing version coming from this one-man band.

"What'll you have?" the bartender shouted above the crowd noise.

Maestro Horsman finished the song to loud applause, whistling, and cheering and was teasing a table of women sitting near the stage. Zach took advantage of the relative quiet to make introductions.

"Hap," he said to the bartender, "this is Gatlin from

Rhode Island. And this is Hap, the Dean of Bartenders in Okoboji."

"I'll have a Bud Light," Gat said.

"Make it two," Zach added.

A blonde and a redhead entered the back door and it was easy to tell from the relieved looks on their faces that they had been the alley screamers from a few minutes before.

Hap returned with the drinks just as the blonde and redhead walked past and melted into the crowd. Gat looked, but Hap and Zach gawked.

"I believe our prayers have been answered," Hap said.

"And then some," Zach replied.

The blonde was voluptuous and ample, with a well-developed bosom, tiny waist, and great ass. She had a Marilyn Monroe face and cotton-like platinum blonde hair. Maybe she knew it and maybe she didn't, but she could make a living posing as a Marilyn Monroe look-alike at conventions and private parties. She wore a tight white dress that came six inches above her knees and it was cinched tightly by a cream colored belt that helped magnify the curves of her body.

And the redhead, oh, the redhead. She was tall and slender with long legs that went all the way up to her neck. She wore a black leather bustier, skimpy black leather shorts, and knee-high black leather boots with stiletto heels. Her shoulder length fire engine red hair had been teased to the point where it was almost perfectly round – a fire engine red Afro style, almost.

"Quite a pair," Zach said. "One could love you to death

and the other one could beat you to death."

Hap thought for a moment. "I'll take the beating," he said.

"Did you hear the first clue?" Zach asked Hap.

"Ya, but like most of them it makes no sense to me," Hap said. "But, I've got one for you fellas – A guy walks into a bar; what does he say?"

"Give me a beer," Zach said.

"Randy?" Hap said to a husky guy standing next to Zach.

"Give me a shot of whiskey," Randy replied.

"Nope," Hap said, "a guy walks into a bar and says – 'Ouch.'"

"That's lame, Hap," Randy said.

"Did Punky get hold of you?" Hap asked Zach. "He called here about five times looking for you."

"He made me promise to call and give him The Clue immediately after it was read by Mayor Mitchell, and I did. I left the message on his cell phone, which he often forgets to turn on or often doesn't check for messages. If he quit calling here it must have eventually dawned on him that he should check his cell phone. It won't do him any good anyway. Nobody could figure out the riddle from the first clue."

Maestro Horsman gave them what they came for – rousing classic Rock 'N Roll. There was "Real, Real Gone," by Van Morrison, "Brandy," by Looking Glass, "Can't Buy Me Love," by the Beatles, and "Runaway," by Del Shannon.

"Before I take a break, I've got a riddle for you," The

Maestro announced. "What is the most honorable music instrument?"

"A drum," someone yelled. "Electric guitar," shouted another. "Trombone," "Kazoo," "Wazoo," "Tuba," "French Horn," "Clarinet . . . ."

"Who in the hell said *Clarinet* as the most honorable musical instrument?" The Maestro asked scanning the crowd.

"Well, the most honorable musical instrument is the… *Upright Piano*," he said before leaving the stage to a mixed chorus of laughter, moans, groans, and a couple of boos.

"We caught his eye when we walked by," the redhead said to the blonde.

"I think we did more than catch his eye," the blonde replied, "we filled it and damn near ripped it out."

"And did you see the bartender and that other guy drooling?" the redhead asked. "I feel sorry for their wives or girlfriends tonight."

"Did you smell his cologne?" the blonde asked. "I think it was *Creed Bois du Portugal,* Mmmmm!"

"Or it could have been *Rance Le VanQueur,* Mmmmm!" the redhead said.

"Whatever it is, I'd like to lick . . .," the blonde started.

"Easy girl, easy," the redhead said with a smile. "There will be plenty of time for that, and more, later."

The crowd was abuzz, with at least half the conversation centering on The Clue. Some delved into the various possible meanings of the word, *fall.* Others were deciphering the many potential interpretations of other words in The Clue

– focusing mainly on *small, true,* and *majesty.* In the end it seemed everyone resigned themselves to the fact that no matter how much they debated, speculated, and hypothecated, they had no clue to what The Clue meant, so the only sensible thing to do was to wait for the next clue tomorrow and to go ahead and party tonight.

Maestro Horsman returned to the stage. "I'll give you guys one more chance," he said. "Here's another riddle – All four members of this rock group are dead, including one who was assassinated. Who is it?"

Names of rock bands, many of whom are still very much alive and rockin', and others that never existed in the first place, flew through the air, "The Beatles," "The Doors," "Jimi Hendrix," "John Lennon," "The Strawberry Raspberries," "Curt Cobain and the Commodores," "Janis Joplin and the Full Tilt Boogie Band," "Frank Sinatra . . . ."

"Whoa," The Maestro yelled. "Who in the hell said Frank Sinatra? You should be banned from repeating the words, Rock 'N Roll, ever again and should be sentenced to listening to Barry Manilow records around the clock for forty-eight hours straight. Now, here's the answer to the riddle about the four members of this rock group who are dead – you'll hate yourselves for missing it – the answer is - *Mt. Rushmore.*"

The Maestro tore into Sam Cooke's "Another Saturday Night" before the crowd had a chance to verbally abuse him.

"I'm going to move along," Gat said to Zach as he downed the final swig of his Bud Light.

"Thanks for the beer," Zach replied.

Gat weaved his way through the crowd in Ruebins and exited the front door. There was still a line of over thirty people waiting to get in.

"Thanks for coming," the doorman holding the crowd back said as he looked at Gat curiously as if to say, "I see you coming out, but why didn't I see you going in?"

"I enjoyed the music," Gat said.

"I'm Jim Hentges," he said.

"Gatlin Guthrie from Rhode Island," Gat replied.

Jim leaned close to Gat and spoke softly with a smile tugging at his lips. "Next time, just tap me on the shoulder and I'll let you in no matter how long the line is – you could get mugged out there in that alley."

Gat started to cross the street to make his way back to the Four Seasons Motel when a voice rang out behind him, "Gat, Gatlin." It was Zach.

"There's one more band you should see before you call it a night. The Fishheads are playing right here at Captain's Getaway, and they're great," he said motioning to the bar next to Ruebins.

Gat joined Zach on the sidewalk and they listened to the band through the open windows for a moment. They were playing an up-tempo version of Patsy Cline's "I Fall To Pieces" with a Calypso beat. It was the best version of the song that Gat had ever heard – a real toe-tapper.

There were forty or fifty people waiting in line to get into Captain's, but Zach said, "follow me," as he walked to the head of the line. He whispered a couple of words to the doorman and the doorman stepped aside to let Zach and Gat enter, without paying a cover charge.

"He's a friend of mine," Zach explained about the doorman. "Sometimes us locals have to stick together."

Captain's Getaway is divided into two bar areas, with a design and upbeat atmosphere similar to what you might find in a nightclub in Florida. The front bar is a great place to have a drink or a meal while carrying on a conversation. The back bar is the party area with the band and dance floor. Zach and Gat headed straight to the back area, which was packed with people of all ages.

The Fishheads were a good-time band, playing one up-tempo party song after another. Great songs to sing along with and great to dance to. What more could the crowd ask for!

The guitar player broke a string and the lead singer adlibbed while the guitar player searched his guitar case for another string.

"What is the greatest single use of pigskin worldwide?" the lead singer asked.

"Footballs," someone yelled. "Women's purses," said another. "Shoes," "Gloves," "Leather skirts," "Golf club bags," "Automobile seats," "Baseballs." The answers were coming out of left field.

"Well, the biggest single use of pigskin worldwide, is to ...cover pigs," the singer said. This was, predictably, met with a chorus of boos.

"I'll give you another chance," the singer said while he waited for the guitar player to tune his guitar. "Name a word that rhymes with purple."

"Hurdle," someone shouted.

"It has to be an *exact rhyme,* like 'cat' and 'hat' – not a *near* rhyme like 'cat' and 'mutt,' " the lead singer said. "Hurdle is a *near rhyme.*"

Most people wouldn't know the difference between an exact rhyme and a near rhyme, nor would they care. But to a songwriter or a musician, the difference is immense - often revealing the difference between an amateur and a professional.

"Brittle," someone shouted. "Tittle," said another. "Burp," "Dribble," "Myrtle," "Puddle . . ."

"Hold it, hold it," the singer said. "Most of those aren't even *near rhymes.* But, you're forgiven because there isn't any word in the English language that is an exact rhyme to the word, purple."

"How about *maple surple?*" a guy at the bar yelled.

"A valiant try, my friend," the singer said. "Jason," he yelled to the bartender, "give him a drink on me."

The band went on break after another half dozen songs and Gat took it as his cue to head back to his motel. He bid Zach farewell and thanked him for being his guide for the evening.

Gat exited Captain's Getaway and noticed that some of the same people who were there when Zach and he entered Captain's were still standing in line to get in. He expected that they might give him an evil stare or shout obscenities at him for having jumped the line, but they seemed to be having a good time talking and singing with each other and with a blonde and a redhead who had joined their ranks.

Gat covered the five blocks along Lakeshsore Drive from the Central Emporium to the Four Seasons Resort in about five minutes – a pretty brisk clip. Too brisk for someone in stiletto heels to keep up.

Chapter

6

The Dry Dock is a bar and restaurant attached to the Four Seasons Motel. Originally, the space now occupied by the Dry Dock had been several motel rooms, but converting them to the Dry Dock changed the Four Seasons from a motel into a bona fide resort.

The Four Seasons Resort rests on the east shore of West Lake Okoboji and is known for its view of dazzling sunsets. The Dry Dock is one of only a half dozen bars or restaurants in Okoboji where a boater can pull right up to the dock, tie up, and be sitting at the bar in a minute or two.

The Dry Dock, like most of the bars and restaurants in Okoboji, is casual, where more burgers are served than steaks and more beers are served than martinis. On a normal summer day, the outside deck is packed from before noon until after midnight. Inside seating, which makes the Dry Dock just as popular in the frigid winter months as it is in the summer, provides a panoramic view of the lake through large windows to the west and north.

After enduring shoulder-to-shoulder crowds and amplified music for the past several hours, Gat welcomed the relative quiet of the Dry Dock. There was one empty stool at the bar and Gat slid in.

"I'm Neal," the bartender said. "What can I get you?"

"Just a cola, please," Gat replied.

"I saw you checking into the motel this afternoon," the man sitting on the bar stool next to him said. "I'm Deano."

"*The* Deano?" Gat asked. "Deano from the *Okoboji* novel?"

"That's me," Deano said with a broad grin. "There's hardly a day that goes by in the summer when someone doesn't ask me that – and I've probably autographed a couple hundred books. Some people have gone around and collected the autographs of all the locals included in the story. Probably doesn't make the book worth any more, but just a bunch of small-town folks trying to have a little fun."

"You built the Four Seasons Resort and you're Mayor Mitchell's father, right?" Gat asked.

"Right," Deano replied proudly.

"And, your lady friend from the book – was she real or fictitious?" Gat asked.

"As real as they come," Deano said as he swiveled around in his bar stool to face a group of four women sitting at a round table behind them. "Jody," he said, "come here. There's someone I'd like you to meet."

She had short auburn hair, sparkling dark eyes, and a brilliant smile.

"This is the guy from Rhode Island who's staying at the motel – Gatlin," Deano said. "He knew all about us before he even got to Okoboji."

"Well, it's a pleasure. I hope you enjoy your stay," Jody said.

They visited for a few moments about the evening's activities and about events coming up on the weekend before Jody excused herself and returned to her friends at the table.

"There's a lot of colorful people in this town," Gat said.

"A resort community draws them, or maybe it changes normal people into them," Deano said. "Apparently you've met some of them. And, there's another one of our colorful characters sitting right beside you.

"Marv," Deano said to the man sitting to Gat's right, "this is Gatlin from Rhode Island. He's visiting Okoboji for a few days."

The white hair and wrinkles were evidence that he had some miles on him, but the sparkle in his eyes, brilliant smile, and vice grip handshake could easily have belonged to a man two decades younger.

"If you want to know anything about anybody in Okoboji, ask Marv. He's a walking encyclopedia of Okoboji history," Deano said.

"Well, I've lived in Okoboji all my life and I used to be in the newspaper business, so I've had a natural curiosity to know everything about everybody who has come and gone in Okoboji," Marv said.

"I stopped at The Gardens for a cocktail this afternoon

and met four guys – Zach, Dick Dick, Sleepy, and Lenny," Gat said. "They seemed like a pretty colorful bunch."

"Zach was sitting at the bar on the third stool and the other three were sitting at a corner table in the back playing cards with another guy, Punky," Marv stated. "Right?"

"Right, but how did you know?" Gat asked.

"That's their routine every Thursday, just like clock-work," Marv said.

"Except Punky wasn't there," Gat said. "Zach said Punky partied hard last night and wasn't able to make it out tonight."

"That must have ruined the fun for Dick Dick, Sleepy, and Lenny," Marv said.

"How's that?" Gat asked.

"Well, Punky's kind of their whipping boy," Marv said. "He's one of those guys who's so smart that he's stupid, and they just love trying to get the best of him."

"Zach told me a little bit about himself – that he's a Jack of all trades and that he loves Okoboji. But the other three guys didn't say too much about themselves, other than that they call themselves The Three Wise Men in the treasure hunt," Gat said.

"A lot of people refer to those three – Dick Dick, Sleepy, and Lenny as the *Okoboji Mafia*. It's all in jest, but there's a grain of truth to it," Marv said.

"Now Punky, on the other hand, that's a different story. His name is Punky Cox. I think his real name is Lee Roy or ElRoy or something like that but everybody's called him

Punky since he was a little kid, because he was such a punk, I guess."

"Is he from around here?" Gat asked.

"Originally, his family was from some small town near Sioux City - Hawarden, I think. In Iowa. Back in the 1920's Punky's great-grandfather was a mechanic at the Chevrolet dealership and Punky's great-grandmother did sewing alterations for the local clothing stores. They were a hard working family with four kids, barely getting by.

"Punky's great-grandfather was a tinkerer, always trying to invent something, but every time he came up with a brilliant new idea he found out that somebody else had already invented it.

"He was reading the newspaper one night while Punky's great-grandmother was doing some sewing and mumbling and grumbling about how the thread always got stuck and didn't feed right and how she always had to untangle it and start over. Well, to make a long story short, Punky's great-grandfather invented a new bobbin for sewing machines that fed thread smoothly without getting stuck or tangled.

"He got a patent on his new bobbin and sold it to every major sewing machine manufacturer of the day including White, Singer, and the companies that made sewing machines for Sears Roebuck. Instead of selling it outright for cash, though, he sold it to them on a royalty basis. Punky said that he earned twenty-five cents for every bobbin. That may not sound like much, but remember this was in the 1920's and every self-respecting wife and mother owned a sewing machine and knew how to use it and wore one out about every five or ten years. The 1920's through the 1950's were the heydays for sewing machines and millions of Punky's great-grandfather's bobbins were sold, at twenty-five cents each. And, that was back when twenty-five cents was worth twenty-five cents. Back in a time when a good man's wages was maybe a dollar a day."

"So Punky's great-grandfather made millions," Gat said.

"Right, and he invested wisely, mostly buying farms and post office buildings that he leased to the U.S. Postal Department," Marv said.

"So Punky inherited a fortune," Gat said.

"Well, yes and no," Marv said. "Have you ever heard the saying, 'From shirtsleeves to shirtsleeves in three generations'?"

"I don't think so," Gat replied.

"What it means is that Granddaddy was a sharp old bird who rolled up his sleeves and worked like a dog from sunup to sundown and amassed a fortune. Then, his son comes along who is a lazy ne'er-do-well who doesn't think he has to work because he's rich and can live off of his father's money - and there's so much money that even the son can't spend it all, so no problem. Then the grandson, the third generation, who is a nincompoop, comes along and ends up blowing what's left of the family fortune. And guess what, the family has to roll up its shirtsleeves and has to go back to work. From shirtsleeves to shirtsleeves in three generations."

"And Punky's the fourth generation," Gat said.

"Right," Marv said.

"So Punky's broke?" Gat asked.

"Not broke, but he's not fabulously wealthy like the family once was," Marv said. "For one thing, his great-grandfather had four children, so the original fortune got cut up into four pieces. Then, Punky's grandfather had three kids, so it got cut up further. But still, Punky's father inherited twenty or thirty million. He bought Punky and his sister fancy sports cars and sent them to the finest schools, mostly to get them out of his hair so he could do the wild thing. He was married three or four times and the divorces cut into the fortune a bit, too.

"Punky's grandfather owned a huge house on West Lake Okoboji on what's called the *Gold Coast*," Marv continued. "It was the first really prestigious area on West Lake where all of the families that got rich in banking, manufacturing, and hotels lived. It's still a good address, but other areas of the lake have surpassed it in terms of mansions. Punky inherited the house and lives there alone, but it's pretty much like it was fifty years ago and could use some work."

"Did Punky ever work?" Gat asked.

"Punky was a professional student. He got kicked out of four or five colleges back east and down south, flunked out of a couple more, and transferred voluntarily another half dozen times before he finally found his crowd at Berkley in California," Marv explained. "He went to college about fifteen years and has degrees in Philosophy, Psychology, Sociology, Anthropology, Theology, and Latin, among other things. He's got a lot of knowledge, in theory, but he's never been able to apply it to anything. He lives off of a trust fund or some rental income or something like that and basically engages in philosophical conversations in coffee houses and bars as a daily way of life."

"So, do the other guys, The Three Wise Men, resent him for being so well educated?" Gat asked.

"They don't resent him for all of his education, but it perturbs them that sometimes Punky comes across as an intellectual snob," Marv said.

"To get even one time they made up T-shirts with the slogan, *PUNKY COX'S COLLEGE CAREER*, listing every college Punky had attended with a check mark in front of each one. There were over a dozen colleges. They thought it was hilarious and gave away about a hundred of them to unsuspecting tourists who promised to wear them. That was a couple of years ago and it was probably the turning point where Punky finally figured out the contempt that his so-called friends had for him."

"And The Three Wise Men?" Gat asked

"Their backgrounds are also unique," Marv said. "Sleepy's dad came from a very poor family in South Dakota. When he was in his mid twenties Sleepy's dad worked as a farm hand, which paid very little. He and a couple of buddies scraped up enough money to go to the South Dakota state fair in Huron for a couple of days. There was a dance one night and there was this one girl who was the homeliest thing that these poor boys had ever seen, just sitting there by herself all night long.

"As a joke, the other boys said they'd pay Sleepy's dad a dollar if he danced with her for two dances. Well, a dollar was a lot of money to a guy like Sleepy's dad and he went for it.

"The girl was so homely that he had to shut his eyes when he danced with her and after sitting there all night by herself she was eager to talk and rattled on and on nonstop. At first Sleepy's dad tried to shut out her endless chatter but the more she talked, the more he found what she said to be interesting if not downright fascinating. First, he learned that her name was Hilda. Second, she had never had a date in her life. Third, she was hungry for a man. Fourth, her father's name was Steven Southworth and he owned a dozen banks. Fifth, she was an only child. And the more she talked the prettier she got. By the end of the second dance Sleepy's dad made a decision, he would marry this girl's dad's money.

"Banker Southworth had been resigned to the fact that his only daughter would never marry and that he would go to his grave without the blessing of having grandchildren and worse than that, there would be no one to carry on the honorable Southworth name.

"When Hilda brought Sleepy's dad home for a visit, Banker Southworth welcomed him with open arms. Oh, I forgot to mention this - Sleepy's dad's name was actually Bill Smith.

"Two weeks later, when Bill Smith and Hilda announced their engagement, Banker Southworth shot his new son-in-law-to-be a deal. If he would change his name to Southworth, he'd make him a vice president at one of his banks and teach him the banking business. And, if he and Hilda produced a male heir to carry on the Southworth name, Bill and Hilda would inherit all of the banks, which were to be eventually handed down to that male heir. So, that's how Sleepy's dad, Bill Smith, became Stephen Southworth, Jr.

"Sleepy's dad was the first man in the state of South Dakota to ever take his wife's maiden name when he got married, and I think he still holds the distinction of being the only one."

"Did they have any other children besides Sleepy?" Gat asked.

"No, Stephen Southworth, III, better known as Sleepy, is the only child. It is widely believed that Sleepy's parents had sex only one time, which resulted in Sleepy."

"Did Sleepy carry on the Southworth family banking tradition?" Gat asked.

"Sleepy inherited all of his mother's beauty and all of her father's banks," Marv said. "There's still about a dozen of them, including one here in the lakes area."

"Is he a good banker?" Gat asked.

"In spite of his droopy appearance and in spite of himself, Sleepy has been able to at least hang onto most of his grandfather's banking empire. It bugs him, though, that he never accomplished anything on his own, that the only reason he has wealth and position is that he was lucky enough to have the right grandfather."

"Has he ever tried any ventures of his own?" Gat asked.

"Many. He's tried many and they've all flopped. For instance, he invented a Styrofoam beer keg, which sounds like a great idea to keep the beer cold, but they could only survive about two college keggers before they were so beaten up they had to be thrown away.

"Another one was a device called the *Towaway*. Some guy invented this device and started a company to manufacture and sell it, but he ran out of money before he sold even his first one. Sleepy, thinking he spotted a revolutionary product that would become an accessory for every car sold in America, swooped in and bought the device, the manufacturing equipment, the building – the whole shebang.

"The *Towaway* was a towing device that was bolted into the trunk of a medium-sized or full-sized car. The idea was that if you needed to tow a car, you could just open your trunk, unfold this device, hook up, and away you go without calling a tow truck.

"There were three flaws with the *Towaway*," Marv continued. "First, the car that needed the towing was probably the one that had this device in its trunk, so it did you no good. Secondly, trying to pull a car out of the ditch with your car is a good way to rip the rear end out of your car. And, thirdly, if you had the *Towaway* in your trunk, there wasn't room for much else."

"Didn't Sleepy recognize these limitations before he bought the company?" Gat asked.

"He was so convinced that this thing would be the hottest automotive accessory since the cruise control that he put on blinders and refused to even consider the possibility that it might not work," Marv said.

"Was that his worst fiasco?" Gat asked.

"Well, after the *Towaway* flopped, he had that building and he wanted to do something with it rather than leave it sit empty. Sleepy did some research, reading articles in *Moneygrubber* magazine and *Wounded Entrepreneur* magazine and others like that, trying to find something that was unique and that had the potential to earn huge profits.

"Finally, he read this article that seemed to be speaking directly to him, extolling the virtues of operating an ostrich ranch. The article said that an ostrich egg weighed four pounds, was the equivalent of about twenty-five chicken eggs, and could be sold for $45 each. Now, an ostrich will lay 40-100 eggs per year, so Sleepy used the average of that, 70 eggs per year, in his calculations. At 70 eggs a year and $45 each, Sleepy figured that each ostrich could earn around $3,150 a year and in its egg-laying life of 20 years, it could earn about $63,000."

"That's pretty impressive," Gat said.

"You ain't heard nothin' yet," Marv said. "Sleepy discovered that if he hatched the eggs rather than sold them, he could sell a 60-day old chick for about $300. Now, selling 70 chicks per year at $300 each would yield annual income of $21,000 or lifetime earnings of $420,000 – from each ostrich.

"So, Sleepy plunged into the ostrich ranching business and bought two dozen of them at a cost of around $100,000,"

Marv said.

"How did that work out?" Gat asked.

"Well, he was expecting to earn $500,000 a year and at least ten million over their 20-year lifetime," Marv said.

"And . . . ." Gat said.

"First of all, one male was needed for every two females, for breeding, so out of his twenty-four ostriches, only sixteen laid eggs, thus, cutting his projected income by one-third," Marv said. "Next, Sleepy had never seen an ostrich and must have thought that they were about the size of a chicken – but they grow to about eight feet tall and can weigh 400 pounds. So, the barn wasn't big enough to hold them and he had to add on. Also, a 400-pound bird can eat like a horse, so to speak, which Sleepy hadn't counted on. Finally, even though the baby ostriches could be sold for $300 each, there isn't much of a market for them around here, as in none."

"So does Sleepy just stick to banking these days?" Gat asked.

"He still dreams of the big kill where he can show the world what Sleepy Southworth, III was able to do on his own, but I don't think he's had any new projects since the ostrich ranch," Marv said. "But speaking of Sleepy's banks, you really should visit his bank here in Okoboji and observe."

"What would I be observing?" Gat asked.

"If you were going to be around for a while I'd let you find out for yourself, but since you're leaving in a few days, I'll tell you. As you probably noticed, Sleepy is one of the home-liest men on the planet."

"I noticed," Gat replied.

"Well," Marv replied, "Sleepy has two very strict employment policies in his banks – the women hired must be beautiful and the men hired must be uglier than he is."

"So, if it weren't for the arrangement with Hilda's father, Sleepy's name actually would be George Smith or Tom Smith or something like that," Gat said.

"That's right," Marv agreed. "Like they say in South Dakota, if you scratch a Southworth, you'll find a Smith."

"How about Dick Dick?" Gat asked.

"The story of Dick Dick, or as we call him around here, Two Dicks, actually starts with his father, Herbert Dick," Marv said. "Herbie was a fabulous salesman but he always thought small. He sold vacuum cleaners, and ointments, and shoes, and stuff like that and he sold the hell out of them but never made much money.

"Dick Dick was an all state defensive lineman in high school football and played college ball at what is now called Minnesota State University in Mankato, about a hundred miles northeast of here, where he became a Division II All American. There was a lot of speculation that Dick Dick might get drafted into the pros, but in his final college game he suffered a career-ending injury that landed him in the hospital for a couple of weeks. In football he was a bulldozer, which is how he has lived his life, steamrolling anything in his way without any regard for the consequences. He's been rich two times and broke twice. Right now he's rich again.

"His dad, Herbie, was an eternal optimist, thinking that

anything and everything was possible, even in the face of certain disaster. Dick Dick operates the same way and when things are good they're fabulous and when they're bad, they're in shambles. There are two things that you can count on with Two Dicks - sooner or later he'll go broke and sooner or later he will rise again from the ashes and become richer than he ever was before.

"But, rich or poor, Dick Dick's a charmer. Whether he's talking to a client, a prospect, a bus driver, a bartender, or a banker, he's always polishing his sales lingo and always selling. The way he figures it, if he doesn't sell them something today he might sell them something next week or next year, so he's always, always working on his game."

Neal, the bartender interrupted. "Another drink, guys?"

"Bring a round for the three of us," Deano said. "Put it on my tab."

Neal grabbed three drinks and set them up. "I've got a riddle for you guys," he said. "Can you tell me what is the shortest sentence in the English language?"

"Yes," Deano said quick as a flash, "the shortest sentence is, 'Yes.'"

"That's close," Neal said. "But, the shortest sentence is, 'Go.'"

"It figures that Neal would know that," Deano said. "He's a teacher in California and comes back to Okoboji to bartend every summer."

"And the last one of The Three Wise Men, Lenny?" Gat

asked Marv, getting back to the story.

"Lenny's really the only one of the bunch who's almost normal. At least he came from a normal background from a normal family. His father was a used car salesman and his mother was a high school English teacher and debate coach," Marv explained. "Since his mother was the debate coach, Lenny naturally participated in debate and he won all sorts of awards. So, what career should a guy who's a whiz at debating go into? Well, he should become a lawyer and that's what Lenny did.

"He vowed to become an honest lawyer, and he was for a while, but then he became fast friends with Dick Dick and, by most accounts, became a little slippery. And, he's proud of it, I guess – the personalized licensed plate on his Jaguar convertible is *SLICK*. Lenny says that the word, Slick, refers to his car but Sigmund Freud would probably say that subconsciously Lenny was referring to himself."

"I met a lot of other people tonight also," Gat said. "People like the bartenders at The Gardens, Mark and Jennifer, and Hap at Ruebins, and a whole bunch of people from the Rock 'N Roll Museum. Any interesting or unusual stories there?"

"They're all good people," Marv said, "but they're normal - too normal for a bestselling book or movie to be made of their lives and they're too normal for a good barroom story. And that's good; I like normal people."

Marv eased himself off of the bar stool and shook hands with Gat. "I've got to go, but it was a pleasure visiting with you," he said, "and I hope you meet a lot more of Okoboji's colorful characters before you leave town – there are some real beauties!"

"Thanks for the stories," Gat said as Marv turned and headed toward the door.

"I've got another riddle for you two," Neal said to Deano and Gat. "What was the first man-made invention to break the sound barrier?"

"I think I know that one," Gat said. "It was Chuck Yeager in 1947 flying the Bell X-1 when he broke Mach 1."

"Good try, and close," Neal said, "but that's not it. The first man-made invention to break the sound barrier was *the whip*. The crack of the whip is actually the sound of breaking the sound barrier."

"These damn teachers," Deano said with a smile, "they know everything, especially the tricky stuff."

"Can I ask you something?" Gat asked. "Has everybody in this town always been so wrapped in riddles? I mean, everywhere I've gone tonight everybody's asking everybody else a riddle. It's fun, but it's almost weird."

"Nobody even said the word, riddle, or could spell it, in this town for the past fifty years until the Chamber concocted the Great Okoboji Treasure Hunt about four weeks ago," Deano said. "Now everybody's riddle crazy. But mainly it's a matter of pride, trying to solve the riddle before someone else does. Just a bunch of small town folks . . ."

"I know," Gat interrupted, "just a bunch of small town folks trying to have a little fun."

Deano grinned that mile-wide grin and offered his hand for Gat to shake, "Welcome to Okoboji," he said.

❖ ❖ ❖

Gat unlocked the door to his motel room and flipped on the light switch. He removed his money clip, wallet, watch, and ring and laid them on the dresser. He slid open the patio door and walked out on the deck overlooking the lake for a moment of reflection. Even though it was now past midnight, he could see the red and green boat lights still skimming along the water and could hear voices and music coming from the boats.

It had been a whirlwind evening and he had had a very good time. Gat returned to his room, locked the patio door, and closed the curtain. He sat down on his bed and pulled his cell phone from his shirt pocket.

Gat dialed a number from memory and a moment later uttered the words, "Contact has been made."

He quickly deleted the number he had just dialed and turned off his phone.

Gat got undressed and got into bed as a smile crossed his lips.

Chapter

7

The ringing telephone woke Gat. He glanced at the clock through sleepy eyes; it was a quarter to six. In the morning. He surmised that the front office had rung his room by mistake since no one he knew was aware that he was here at the Four Seasons and if they did, they knew better than to call in the middle of the night like this. He pulled the covers over his head and ignored the ringing.

The caller was insistent and after fifteen rings, Gat grabbed the phone, thinking maybe it was some emergency from back home and that they had somehow tracked him down.

"Good Morning, Gatlin," a cheery voice said. "This is Dick Dick; did I get you out of bed?"

Gat mumbled, "I had to get up to answer the phone anyway," as he tried to figure out why Two Dicks would be calling him at this hour, or any hour for that matter.

"I'd like to take you out for breakfast," Dick Dick said.

"Do you always get people out of bed in the middle of

the night like this?" Gat asked.

"Just a habit I developed by being in the real estate business, I guess," Dick Dick said.

"A habit?" Gat asked.

"Our Multiple Listing Service, where all of us Realtors share our listings with each other, has a rule that if a competitor's listing is about to expire, we can't contact the property owner to try to solicit the listing until after it expires. Well, every listing expires at one second after midnight of the final day of the listing period.

"I get up earlier than any other Realtor in Okoboji and to get a listing after it expires, I call people at maybe six in the morning or even five thirty. Hell, I've called people at two seconds after midnight or at two a.m. to get a listing."

"Doesn't that piss people off, getting rolled out of bed in the middle of the night by some damn Realtor?" Gat asked.

"A few of them, yes; but I also get a lot of listings," Dick Dick said. "When they answer the phone and hear those magical words, 'This is Dick Dick from Dick Dick Realty,' it usually mellows them out."

"I'll bet," Gat said.

"So how about it?" Dick Dick said.

"Dick Dick, if you called me at quarter to six to try to sell me a house, forget it," Gat said. "I'm not buying a house in Okoboji. I'm just passing through – remember?"

"Honest, I'm just trying to be a nice guy and take a visitor from out of town, who doesn't know anybody here, out for breakfast," Dick Dick said. "You east coast guys are too suspicious. Around here when someone offers to take you out to breakfast, that's what they mean. And, that's all they mean."

"Sorry," Gat said. "Back east when a Realtor calls and offers to take you out to breakfast or lunch, you have to check every couple of minutes to see if your wallet is missing."

"Oh, we're just a bunch of ol' boys from the country," Dick Dick said. "You don't have to worry about anything like that here. Now, how about if I pick you up at, say, seven."

"Well, I'm up now," Gat said. "Seven will be fine."

Dick Dick silently congratulated himself on his sales acumen. Nobody in Okoboji was a match for him and neither was this Easterner. He had the ability to anticipate any objection that might possibly be raised and to deliver a powerful rebuttal that brought their sales resistance to its knees. And he had done it again. "That ol' Dick Dick charm," he said to himself.

Dick Dick speed dialed a number and the phone rang seven times before it went to the recipient's voice mail. He rang the number again, let it ring six times, and hung up. He did it again and again until finally a weary voice answered.

"Hello," he said.

"Good morning, is this Mr. Sleepy Southworth the Third?" Dick Dick said cheerfully.

"Dick Dick, you prick, you know damn well this is me – you called my phone, didn't you?" he grumbled.

"Well, phase one of the plan is underway," Dick Dick said. "I'm picking Gatlin up at seven and taking him to breakfast."

"Those Easterners get up early," Sleepy said.

"They sure do," Dick Dick agreed.

"I'll round up the money today, just like I said - just in case this thing works," Sleepy said. "That won't take me long – just a couple of keystrokes on the computer. And, while I'm waiting for the Federal Reserve Bank to open, I'll call Punky. I'll let you know if I can maneuver him safely out of the way for the day."

"Good job," Dick Dick said. "I'll meet you at the Barefoot Bar whenever you're able to get there – and don't bring Punky along. Lenny's going to get there early and get us a table."

"See you there," Sleepy said.

Dick Dick speed dialed another number and the call was answered on the second ring.

"Is the plan in motion?" Lenny asked.

"Right on schedule," Dick Dick replied. "I'm picking him up at seven for breakfast. I tried to get his room number from the front desk but they wouldn't tell me, but I know he's got a lakeside room."

"I'll figure it out," Lenny said. "I'm on my way."

❖ ❖ ❖

Lenny crept along the deserted hallway, checking under each doorway for the sign of light. It was six fifteen in the morning and this was a party town. Nobody but nobody would be up unless somebody had phoned them and rolled them out of bed. And there it was – light under the door of room 214. He had found Gatlin Guthrie.

Lenny retreated from the motel as silently as he had entered and walked to his vehicle, a Grey GMC Envoy, which was parked across the street in the Mineral City restaurant parking lot – the perfect vantage point to keep an eye on the Four Seasons Motel. The Jaguar convertible would have been too conspicuous, but the Envoy was perfect for his stakeout – there were a hundred of them in Okoboji and only a discerning eye could tell one from the other.

At precisely five minutes to seven, Dick Dick's white Cadillac Escalade rolled into the Four Seasons parking lot. A moment later Gatlin Guthrie walked out of the motel, Dick Dick blew his horn, Gatlin got in, and they drove away. It was show time for Lenny.

Lenny drove the Envoy across the street and parked in front of the Four Seasons Motel. He entered by the same door he had exited a half hour ago, walking as though he belonged there, like he was on a mission to meet someone that he knew. The hallway was still deserted – too early for the party crowd to be out and about and therefore also too early for the housekeeping staff to be going about their duties.

The Three Wise Men had calculated that Lenny would have a window of opportunity of nearly an hour to do what he had to do before the motel came alive. Step one, getting Gatlin out of the room and step two, finding which room was his, had gone smoothly. Now for the tricky part – step three.

Lenny tiptoed down the hallway to room 214. There

was no light shining under the door. Perfect. Lenny removed a small tool from his pocket and began to work on the lock. Back in college, when he had worked part-time for Iowa City Glass and Locksmith, he could pop open a locked car door in a matter of two minutes and could unlock a house door in three minutes or less. Even though he didn't expect anyone to wander down the hallway at this time of the morning, Lenny worked feverishly – this was the most dangerous part of the entire plan and he didn't want anyone to . . . click, the door handle turned. He was in.

Lenny grabbed the Do Not Disturb sign, hung it on the outside door handle, and quietly closed and locked the door. He stood in the middle of the room and took several deep breaths. The serious nature of his actions hadn't hit him until he was standing in the hallway jimmying the door, which is identified in the Iowa Criminal Code as *Forcible Entry,* or simply in street language, Breaking and Entering.

"What the hell was I thinking?" Lenny whispered to himself. "If I had got caught, I'd have been disbarred and I would have done hard time in the slammer. What the hell was I thinking?"

Had the Great Okoboji Treasure Hunt and all of this riddle solving turned everything in life into one gigantic puzzle to solve? Had Dick Dick's harebrained scheme caused greed to overtake judgment? Had he been swayed by Dick Dick's sales pitch about making quick and easy millions with no risk?

Bilking old widows out of their inheritance was one

thing, but breaking and entering . . . .

"Whoa, whoa," Lenny whispered as he tried to get a grip on himself. What had come over him? What was he thinking? He had to get his mind straight.

"It's not a crime if you don't get caught," he whispered to himself, and he had not gotten caught. Gatlin Guthrie was in the watchful custody of Dick Dick, sitting in a restaurant in Spirit Lake and there was no way that Gatlin would get loose and catch him in the room. The Do Not Disturb sign would keep the housekeeping staff at bay for as long as he needed and there was nothing or nobody to worry about. Lenny smiled to himself as he surveyed the contents of Gatlin's room. For a moment there he had almost lost it, but he was now back to the Lenny that he knew and loved. The one with larceny in his heart.

Lenny carefully opened each drawer of the dresser – nothing. He was about to open the suitcase sitting along the wall when he noticed the leather briefcase on the shelf above the clothes rack. He studied the briefcase's exact location on the shelf so he could put it back precisely as it had been. He checked to see if Gatlin had attached a hair or a piece of tape to the briefcase so he could tell if it had been tampered with. It looked clean. Lenny carefully removed the briefcase, keeping it level so the contents didn't shift. He laid the briefcase on the table and flicked the latches with his thumbs; it wasn't locked. Either there was nothing of value in the briefcase or Gatlin was far more trusting of Midwesterners than he ought to be.

Lenny peered at the contents of the briefcase. There were road maps of Colorado and Kansas, a John Grisham novel, and a legal size yellow notepad with a handwritten itinerary listing his four-day stay in Okoboji, three days in Hutchinson, Kansas, and three days in Pueblo, Colorado.

"So that's where his two potential building sites are for his new project," Lenny thought to himself.

There was a 9" x 12" manila envelope beneath the yellow legal pad and Lenny removed it cautiously. He carefully opened the flap and removed a sheet of paper and unfolded it – jackpot! It was a blueprint for a 150,000 square foot building. The writing at the top said *CONFIDENTIAL – PROPERTY OF THE UNITED STATES GOVERNMENT DEFENSE DEPARTMENT. INTELLIGENCE DIVISION.*

The words almost knocked the wind out of Lenny. This was big-time stuff that Gatlin was involved in. Visions of spies and counterspies and code breakers and wiretaps rattled around in Lenny's brain.

Lenny removed another sheet from the envelope and unfolded it. It was a schematic of the grounds, showing the building in the center with several smaller buildings surrounding it and with what appeared to be a series of fences and barricades separating the parking lots from the buildings. A note in the corner indicated that the layout covered 1,000 acres, which coincidently, was close to the number of acres that Punky and his sister owned.

Lenny carefully removed the final sheet of paper from the envelope and the words on it almost made his knees buckle. He read it a second time, just to be sure.

It was the budget for the project, totaling over nine hundred million dollars. Twenty-two million had been allocated for purchase and preparation of the grounds and the rest was for construction, including architectural fees. Dick Dick had been right; if they could convince Gatlin to build his project in Okoboji, and if they could quickly buy up Punky's land before Gatlin Guthrie found out about it, they could turn millions. And, it would only take them a few days to do it. Lenny was already picking out the color of the Mercedes convertible that he'd buy.

Lenny carefully replaced the contents in the briefcase and put it back on the shelf exactly where it had been. He tiptoed to the door and slowly opened it and stuck his head out. No one was in sight. He quickly placed the Do Not Disturb sign on the inside door handle, stepped out, and closed it behind him. He had done it. He was in the hallway and he was in the clear; it wasn't a crime to be in a motel hallway.

Lenny exited the motel by the same door he had entered and spotted Mayor Mitchell coming from the motel office across the parking lot.

"Good morning, Governor," Lenny shouted to the Mayor. "Have you seen Dick Dick? He said he was going to take that visitor from back east, Gatlin, out for breakfast and I thought I'd join them."

"Haven't seen either one of them," Mayor Mitchell answered.

"Well, I'll probably run into them later," Lenny said.

"Have a good day."

Lenny got in the Envoy and hit the speed dial on his cell phone.

"Dick Dick Realty," the voice on the other end said.

"The sky is clear today and the sun is shining brightly," Lenny said, using a code that they had agreed on. "I heard a rumor that someone is looking for a piece of ground of about one thousand acres. I read it somewhere. I thought you might want to follow up on that."

"I'm with someone now," Dick Dick said, "but I can meet you at my office this afternoon if you like."

"Well then, good day to you Mr. Two Dicks," Lenny said, "see you at the Barefoot Bar at five thirty."

"Next Tuesday will be fine," Dick Dick said into his cell phone. "I'll meet you at my office at 10 a.m. Thanks for calling, Mr. Anderson."

"This is one of the greatest inventions of all time," Dick Dick said to Gatlin, holding up his cell phone. "I can be anywhere doing anything and when people call they think I'm at work in my office, just like that guy."

Dick Dick parked across the street from the Family Diner in downtown Spirit Lake.

"If you like home cookin', this place is great," Dick Dick said as they crossed the street.

The Family Diner is long and narrow with a row of booths running the entire length along one wall and a row of tables running down the center. A couple of additional tables are in the back just inside the entryway. Seating capacity might be seventy-five and the place is normally packed all day long. Even though seating is limited, the service is so fast that tables turn over quickly, so even if the place is packed, one rarely has to wait more than five minutes for a table.

Dick Dick and Gat were in luck. They walked in just as a group of four got up to leave and they grabbed the table. Within seconds the dirty dishes were cleared from the table, it was wiped down, and menus and glasses of water were delivered.

"If you like eggs, hash brown potatoes, sausage, and toast, I'd recommend the Number 4 special," Dick Dick said. "They make their own breakfast sausage here and it's great."

"I'll take your recommendation," Gat said.

As if on cue, the waitress was there to take their orders. "We've got a special today," she said. "If you can answer this riddle in ten seconds you'll get a ten percent discount on your order."

"Lay it on us," Dick Dick said.

"Name three consecutive days without using Monday, Tuesday, Wednesday, Thursday, Friday, Saturday, or Sunday – your ten seconds start now – ten, nine, eight, seven, six…"

"Christmas Day, New Year's Eve, and New Year's Day," Dick Dick blurted out.

"Times up," she said. "And, of course your lousy answer is wrong. The answer is *Yesterday, Today,* and *Tomorrow.*"

"How about giving us another one – double or nothing for your tip," Dick Dick said.

"Dick Dick, I hate to take advantage of the unwitting,

the defenseless, the unarmed, the weak, the inept, the . . . ."

"Just let us have it," Dick Dick said, "double or nothing for your tip."

"I warned you," she said. "Here it is – Before Mount Everest was discovered, what was the tallest mountain in the world? You've got ten seconds."

"Mount Evans, Mount Ranier, Mount McKinley, Mount Ararat, Mount . . . ."

"Time's up," she said. "Before Mount Everest was discovered, the tallest mountain in the world was – *Mount Everest.*"

"Cheap shot," Dick Dick whined.

"It's only a cheap shot if you don't know the answer, Dick Dick," she said. "Now, what would you like?"

"He'll have the Number 4 special and I'll have the Number 3 special," Dick Dick said.

"Have you figured out the treasure hunt riddle from the first clue?" Gat asked.

"No. The first two or three clues are usually so vague that even Einstein couldn't figure it out, let alone The Three Wise Men," Dick Dick said. "But, half the fun's just being a part of the event and getting together with friends and trying to figure it out. But, two weeks ago The Three Wise Men were seconds away from grabbing the treasure – got beat out by some goofy-looking guy who could run faster than we could."

"I remember you guys saying that last night," Gat said.

"Well, it's as close as we've come, or may ever come,

to claiming one of the treasures so we tell the story to anybody who will listen. Since most people have never figured out where any of the treasures were, it seems to give us a little prestige in the treasure hunting community. You know, actually figuring out the riddle and almost grabbing the treasure."

The plates of food were delivered within five minutes of the order being placed, even though the Diner was packed.

Gat looked at his heaping plate of food and his mouth dropped open. The plate was piled high and was overflowing. The serving of hash browns was about six inches long, four inches wide and two inches thick – it looked like a triple order. The patty sausage was about six inches in diameter and over a half inch thick. The two scrambled eggs looked more like five eggs than two. The only part of the order that was close to normal in size was the toast, four pieces.

The food was served on a large plate, but the portions were so huge that the sausage was piled on top of the hash browns and the toast was piled on top of the sausage, which still barely left room for the scrambled eggs.

"This is enough for four people," Gat said. "I can't possibly eat all of this."

"You're in the Midwest now, Gatlin, my friend. We believe in full measure. Eat up," Dick Dick said.

"How come you didn't order the Number 4?" Gat asked.

"Oh, I couldn't possibly eat the Number 4," Dick Dick said with a smile. "That's why I order the Number 3."

Gat was right, he ate all he could but still hardly put a

dent in the plateful.

"I surrender," Gat said. "I've never seen a breakfast that large in my life. It will be a good story to tell the folks back in Rhode Island."

The check came to $16.23, with tax, and Dick Dick slowly and methodically counted out the exact amount, down to the penny, and placed it in the waitress's hand.

"Now behave yourself," the waitress said with a wink as she put the money in the cash register.

"No way," Dick Dick replied as he slipped a $10 tip into her hand.

"Got any plans for the day?" Dick Dick asked as they got into his Escalade.

"No, I'm just going to see the sites, do the tourist thing, enjoy Okoboji – that kind of thing," Gat said.

"Well, then, let me show you around," Dick Dick said.

"Promise you won't try to sell me a house?" Gat said with a smile.

"Maybe a condo, but not a house," Dick Dick said. "Okay, not even a condo. I'll just show you around. I'll be your official tour guide and will show you things that you couldn't possibly see on your own."

"Sounds good. Let's go," Gat said.

Chapter
8

"Good morning, Punky, I didn't get you out of bed, did I?" Sleepy asked.

"Surprisingly, you did not," Punky answered. "I stayed home last night, didn't have a single cocktail, sprang out of bed at the crack of eight this morning, and had a glass of orange juice, straight. Stuff tastes terrible without a little bump."

"What's on your schedule for today?" Sleepy asked.

"You know me," Punky said, "every day's a Saturday. Don't have anything on the schedule until tonight when they reveal the second clue. What do you have in mind?"

"Well, I'm going up to Jackpot Junction and I thought maybe you'd like to go along," Sleepy said.

"Maybe another time," Punky said.

Sleepy had to think fast. Punky was normally willing to go to Jackpot Junction or to any other casino at a moment's notice. And, part of the master plan was to get Punky out of town for the day so Dick Dick could work on Gatlin Guthrie without Punky stumbling onto them and messing everything up, and maybe costing them millions.

"Did you read last week's newsletter from Jackpot?" Sleepy asked.

"I don't think I got one," Punky said.

"Well, they've had a rash of winners at Keno," Sleepy said. "One woman hit seven out of seven for over $6,000 and somebody else hit an eight out of nine and two or three people hit five out of five and six out of six."

"Really!" Punky said. "Maybe they loosened up the machines."

"They must have, otherwise there wouldn't be so many winners all of a sudden," Sleepy said.

"We'll be back in time for the clue?" Punky asked.

"Absolutely. I don't want to miss it either," Sleepy said.

"Well then, let's go," Punky said.

"I'll pick you up in a half hour," Sleepy said.

Sleepy turned off his phone and smiled to himself. He knew that the allure of loose Keno machines would be too strong for Punky to resist, even if it wasn't true.

Keno is a game similar to the lottery. In large casinos, Keno is often played as a live game, operated by casino employees. Whether they have live Keno or not, all casinos have Keno machines where players can play the game by themselves, one-on-one against the machine.

Live Keno is a leisurely game, where a new game is played every five or ten minutes. Many Keno enthusiasts prefer to play the Keno machines instead, because a game can be played in less than thirty seconds. Jackpot Junction does not have live Keno, but it has numerous Keno machines, which Punky prefers anyway because of the rapid pace at which games can be played, thus speeding up the chance of winning, theoretically.

There are 80 numbers on the Keno board, numbered consecutively from 1 to 80. A player selects from three to ten numbers before the game begins. Then, the machine picks 20 numbers at random. The player wins if enough of the numbers they had selected are "hit." For instance, if a player bet a quarter and played three numbers, they would win nothing if zero or one of their numbers is hit, would win one quarter if two numbers are hit, and would win 48 quarters if all three numbers are hit.

Since twenty numbers are drawn, it might seem like it would be impossible *not* to hit all three of your numbers, but the odds are 71.07 to 1 against it. In fact, Keno has one of the poorest odds of winning in the casino, yet people flock to the game because of the potential for a huge payout for a small bet. As an example, if a player hit seven out of seven on a quarter bet, the winnings would be 6,400 quarters or $1,600. If the player had bet four quarters, the maximum on most machines, the winnings would be $6,400. And, that is the appeal of Keno.

Oh, even though the payout is huge - 6,400 quarters for a one quarter bet - the odds are 40,978 to 1 against it happening. It's about what you would expect from a game where you pick your numbers first, and then they pick their numbers.

Punky was aware of the odds of winning at Keno and

was aware that it represented one of the worst games in the casino, percentage wise. And, that was part of what appealed to him about Keno. It was a game that was so hard to win at that when he did win, it reconfirmed his belief that he, Punky Cox, who was smarter than most humans, was also smart enough to outwit a Keno machine.

Jackpot Junction is a casino about a hundred miles north of Okoboji on the Lower Sioux Indian Reservation in Minnesota. The casino is out in the country, about three miles south of Morton and five miles east of Redwood Falls.

Even before the days of the casino, you could drive through the Lower Sioux Reservation and never know that you were actually on an Indian reservation. There were only a few dozen houses and there was little to distinguish those houses from others in the area that were not on the reservation.

Many years before the casino came into existence, the Native American Indians living on the Lower Sioux Reservation had become integrated into the community. They held jobs in the stores and factories in surrounding towns and some owned and operated their own businesses. Their children attended the public schools, and they attended the same churches as the white people in the community. They were a normal part of the community in virtually every way.

In 1984, a provision in federal law allowing gambling on Indian reservations was exploited and a small bingo hall was established on the Lower Sioux Reservation. The bingo hall was wildly successful and it was soon expanded.

In 1988, a small room was added to the bingo hall and a few slot machines and two blackjack tables were installed. They were a huge hit from the very beginning and soon a larger room was added for more slot machines and table games.

Jackpot Junction grew rapidly and the building additions became larger and fancier. You would think a casino that was expanded by adding a room here and a room there and another room over there would have the same appearance as one of those neat old country churches that had four or five uncoordinated building additions with pieces sticking out in all directions. But, that wasn't true. Each addition to Jackpot Junction was well thought out and was coordinated to fit the existing structure with an end result that was attractive and functional.

Jackpot Junction became the largest casino in America between Las Vegas and Atlantic City. Keep in mind that this was a casino located in the middle of cornfields three miles from Morton, Minnesota, population, 410, and five miles from Redwood Falls, Minnesota, population, 5,459. The only metropolitan area with sizable population for three hundred miles in any direction is the twin cities of Minneapolis and Saint Paul, well over a hundred miles away.

The success of Jackpot Junction can be attributed to a couple of business principles that have been tried and tested and proven true in the free enterprise system in America – Give 'em what they want and market the hell out of it to let 'em know that you've got it.

On a regular daily basis, tour buses loaded with eager

gamblers arrived at Jackpot Junction from as far away as Chicago and Nashville and everywhere in between. It was common for 40 or 50 buses, each with a capacity of 47 passengers, to arrive daily. In addition, scores of gamblers from hundreds of miles away drove their own vehicles. Add to that the locals from within 40 or 50 miles and you've got the hottest hot spot within two thousand miles in any direction.

"You actually look pretty good this morning," Sleepy said as Punky got into the car.

"I haven't had a drink for nearly a day and a half and I'm learning one thing - this sobriety ain't all it's cracked up to be," Punky said.

"Amen, brother," Sleepy agreed.

Some psychologists have a theory that everything a person does is a quest to maintain, enhance, and display his or her self-concept so that others will see them in the same way that they see themselves. Thus, if a man views himself as being athletic, he might wear a shirt with a football team name on it, wear a baseball cap bearing the logo of another team, and drive around with a bicycle or kayak on the top of his four-wheel drive while he chugs down a sports drink.

Punky Cox is living proof that the psychologists' theory might actually be true. He is a slender man with round wire-rimmed glasses, a mustache, and neatly trimmed hair. Even in the summer, except for days when the temperature exceeds eighty degrees, he can be seen driving around Okoboji in his Austin Healey roadster with the top down wearing his seven-piece driving cap and tweed sport coat with leather patches on the elbows. From his appearance it is easy to surmise that this man is either an intellect, or some weirdo who is vainly trying to relive his glory days on campus. And, in reality, both of these observations would be correct.

I've got a riddle for you," Punky said. "What two states have their state's name in their capitol?"

"That's not a riddle, that's a history quiz, or a government test," Sleepy said.

"Give up?" Punky asked.

"I surrender," Sleepy said.

"Oklahoma City and Indianapolis," Punky said with a tinge of superiority in his voice.

"Okay, here's one for you," Sleepy said. "A magician threw a ball that was untouched by anyone or anything. The ball stopped by itself, reversed its direction, and returned to the magician. How did the magician do it?"

"He had one of those rubber bands attached to the ball – a small one that was invisible," Punky answered.

"The ball was untouched by anyone or anything," Sleepy restated.

"He threw it against a wall," Punky said.

"Again I say, the ball was untouched by anyone or anything," Sleepy said. "Give up?"

"Not yet. I'm thinking," Punky said.

They drove in silence for five minutes while Punky tried to work out the answer, screwing up his face, wringing his hands, and making sweeping motions in the air with his arms and hands. Finally, he surrendered. "I give up."

"You're gonna kick yourself," Sleepy said with a smile. "The magician threw the ball straight up in the air."

"I could kick myself," Punky said.

The journey passed quickly as they exchanged riddles, very few of which were solved.

As they pulled into the Jackpot Junction parking lot Punky said, "All of a sudden, just now, this feeling of incredible luck has come over me."

"They will curse the moment we arrived and will bless the moment we depart," Sleepy said.

Chapter

9

If there was one thing that Dick Dick knew, it was Okoboji. He knew every subdivision, every bay of every lake, every development, and every piece of ground in the entire region consisting of Spirit Lake, Okoboji, Arnolds Park, and Milford. And, he drove Gat through every one of them, keeping up an endless chatter exalting the virtues of every property that they viewed.

Gat recalled what Deano had told him – Dick Dick was always selling and was always polishing his sales skills regardless of where he was, who he was talking to, and what he was doing. Gat had witnessed it in Dick Dick's interaction with the waitress at the Family Diner and he was witnessing it again now, first hand, as the object of Dick Dick's sales tactics. Even though Dick Dick had promised not to try to sell him anything, Gat knew that every word that Dick Dick said and every move he made was carefully designed to eventually try to manipulate him into buying something, somewhere in Okoboji.

Dick Dick drove south on Highway 71 through Arnolds Park and turned west at the stoplight at 202nd street. He drove past C & C Screen Printing and stopped at the stop sign by the Taco House. He turned right and turned off on a short street with a cul-de-sac a short distance from a big sign saying, *CITY OF WEST OKOBOJI*. He stopped the Escalade and they got out.

"Right here, we're in the town of West Okoboji," Dick Dick said. "On the other side of the highway, right over there, is the town of Arnolds Park, and to the south of that street we drove on, 202nd Street, is the town of Milford. It's all very confusing and probably ninety percent of the people living in the Okoboji area couldn't tell you where one town ends and another one starts.

"Well, that's apparently what the city council of West Okoboji thought so they erected this huge sign to make damn sure people knew they were passing through, or at least going past, the town of West Okoboji when they were flying down Highway 71.

"Now, in addition to giving you a little background information on the area, I have a purpose in driving you to this exact spot and telling you all of this," Dick Dick said.

"What's that?" Gat asked.

Dick Dick removed a piece of paper from his pocket and unfolded it. "Remember that set of clues that Sleepy read last night for the Great Okoboji Treasure Hunt?"

"I remember," Gat said. "There were four or five clues."

Dick Dick read them again.

"Clue Number One:

    I may or may not be the best,

    But I think I am the largest.

    You probably cast a glance my way,

    When you whizzed past me the other day.

Clue Number Two:

    From time to time you probably heard my name,

    But didn't know where I was 'till along I came.

    East, west, north, and south,

    Three of these will help you out.

Clue Number Three:

    A little off the beaten road,

    In a circle around you'll go.

    It doesn't have to be that way,

    Stop, get out, take a walk north, I say.

Clue Number Four:

    Slow down,

    When you come into town.

    Even though this is all for fun,

    Don't laugh 'cause my bottom weighs many a ton.

Clue Number Five:

    Paul Simon was loved like this,

    Talkin' about my bottom, that is.

    There's 70 or 80 of me,

    How many clues do you need?"

"Well?" Dick Dick asked.

"Paul Simon sang a song, 'Love Me Like A Rock,'" Gat said. "Was the treasure hidden among those large rocks at the bottom of the *CITY OF WEST OKOBOJI* sign?"

"You're a natural," Dick Dick said. "See, those riddles aren't so hard once you get all the clues put together.

"This is the puzzle that The Three Wise Men solved and were beaten out of the treasure by that goofy guy. He was just getting out of his car when he saw us pull onto this street. He ran like an Olympic sprinter for those rocks and we were on his heels. He started looking around the rocks on the east side of the pile and we started on the west – the treasure was on the east side. End of story."

"There were probably, what – two or three thousand teams or individuals seeking the treasure that week?" Gat asked.

"Probably four or five thousand," Dick Dick said.

"Well, coming in second out of four or five thousand isn't too bad," Gat said.

"No it ain't," Dick Dick said with a wide grin, "No it ain't."

Gat knew that was exactly the observation that Dick Dick was maneuvering him to state so that Dick Dick could bask in his praise for coming in second in the treasure hunt. Gat was happy to play along and was looking forward to the next round, whatever that might be.

Real Estate Sales Trick Number Seventeen isn't in any official handbook or textbook and it isn't openly discussed by people in the real estate profession, but every real estate salesperson worth their salt knows it and uses it. It works like this: The real estate salesperson asks a prospective buyer a series of questions to find out their needs and wants before showing them any property. The salesperson starts out by showing the prospect a series of properties that are too big, too small, too overpriced, too expensive, or in a lousy location. Then, when the prospect is feeling deflated and starting to think that they'll never find what they're looking for, the real estate salesperson springs the trap on them. They show the prospect one final property – and it's absolutely perfect, just what they were looking for. It was, of course, the property that the salesperson had in mind all along but to make sure that the prospect recognized that, they showed them poorly suited properties first to get their mind straight.

Gat suspected that Dick Dick had been baiting the trap all day long and was about to spring it.

Dick Dick turned the Escalade west on Highway 86 and kept up a steady commentary as they drove past Oh Shucks! Bait Shop, Vugteveen Lawn Service, Emerson Bay, and Heather Ridge. Just past Millers Bay, he turned left and drove two miles until he came to a gravel road and turned right. He went one mile and stopped in front of a large sign that said, "Industrial Site – 960 Acres – Dick Dick Realty."

Dick Dick smiled to himself. Lenny had worked fast and had done a good job. He doubted the paint was even dry, but it looked great – very official.

"Here's an industrial site that I've got listed for sale,"

Dick Dick said. "It's an extraordinarily unique site in that it has a clay and sand base and it's flat as a pancake. A builder won't even have to grade it; they can just build on it as it lies."

Gat pondered Dick Dick's words for a moment. "Really?" he said.

Dick Dick had showed Gatlin numerous houses and condominiums and he had showed polite interest at best, but now Dick Dick's trained eyes and keen ears detected a glimpse of genuine interest.

"That's a section and a half," Gat observed. "Is there a road that runs through it on the section line?"

"That's unique, too," Dick Dick said. "It's an *unimproved* road that receives no grading, no graveling, and no snowplowing from the county. It's only an access road to the adjacent sections. I've cleared it with the County Engineer – the county would gladly deed the road back to the two adjoining parcels of land, at no cost, just to get rid of the liability. So, the entire 960 acres would actually be one piece of land with no county roads or easements running through it."

"What's the asking price?" Gat asked.

Dick Dick controlled his excitement – he was leading this Easterner right where he wanted him, as easily as leading a calf with a ring through his nose. "Twenty million," he said nonchalantly, as though he dealt with numbers like that every day. He watched for Gatlin's reaction. He didn't flinch. It was obvious that he actually did deal with numbers like that every day.

"Who owns it?" Gat asked.

"It's owned by a Land Trust," Dick Dick said. "As you probably know, in a Land Trust the identity of the individual owners isn't revealed. It allows individuals to accumulate parcels of ground anonymously without arousing curiosity or suspicion and . . . ."

"I'm familiar with Land Trusts," Gat interrupted. "Just out of curiosity, is there any wiggle room in that twenty million?"

"The Land Trust has already turned down a significant offer, but I can't reveal the exact amount," Dick Dick said. Lying with a straight face had never been a problem for him.

"Is the trustee for the Land Trust in the community?" Gat asked.

Dick Dick knew that this question would be asked for only one reason – that a buyer wanted to know if an offer to buy the land could be acted upon quickly. "The trustee is in the area and has a power of attorney to handle any and all business transactions on behalf of the Land Trust," Dick Dick said.

"Just curious," Gat said.

"Just curious, my ass," Dick Dick said to himself. He could sense that, with his superb salesmanship, and maybe a little fib or two, he had hooked this hotshot east coast developer and now all he had to do was to reel him in. But before he could close in for the kill, he needed more information. He still didn't know what Gatlin Guthrie was up to, other than that Lenny had said it would require about a thousand acres of land. He was eager to park Gatlin somewhere safe for a few hours where Punky Cox wouldn't stumble upon him so he could get together with Lenny and find out what else he had learned by rummaging through Gatlin's motel room.

Dick Dick retraced his route on the gravel roads and returned to Highway 86. He continued north on 86 past the Okoboji View Golf Course and some of the most fabulous lakeside homes in the lakes area until he came to Highway 9. He turned east, heading for Spirit Lake.

"Well, Gatlin, we have now come full circle," Dick Dick said as they pulled into Spirit Lake. "I have an appointment in a half hour so if it's okay with you, I'll drop you at the Four Seasons."

"Absolutely perfect," Gat replied. "I want to take a little walk and explore some of the shops down by the amusement park."

That was also perfect with Dick Dick. Most of the locals waited for the huge sales after Labor Day to do their shopping, so today the gift shops would be crowded with tourists, none of whom would be familiar enough with the local real estate market or Punky's land to mess things up for him.

Seconds after Dick Dick dropped Gatlin off at the Four Seasons Motel he hit the speed dial on his phone. "Lenny," he said, "meet me at my office in five minutes."

Chapter
10

Dick Dick could tell from the look on Lenny's face that he had big news to report.

"It's huge," Lenny said as he spread his hands wide. "Huge."

"Tell me about it," Dick Dick said eagerly.

"Well, I snuck down the hallway and jimmied the lock in about two minutes flat," Lenny began. "I checked every dresser drawer – nothing. Then, I was about to check his suitcase when I noticed a briefcase sitting on a shelf above the clothes rack. I carefully took it down, making sure nothing shifted inside the briefcase. Then, I put the briefcase on the table and . . ."

"Cut the crap," Dick Dick said impatiently. "What did you find?"

"Okay, this is where it gets good anyway," Lenny said. "There was a blueprint of a large building - 150,000 square feet – and several smaller buildings around it, with a fence and some barricades separating the buildings from the parking."

"A hundred fifty thousand square feet – are you sure?" Dick Dick asked.

"Positive," Lenny said. "I read it three times just to be sure and the measurements were 200 feet by 750 feet."

"That's a big building," Dick Dick said. "It would be bigger than three football fields."

"But that's not even the good part," Lenny said. "The heading on the blueprint said, *'CONFIDENTIAL - PROPERTY OF THE UNITED STATES DEFENSE DEPARTMENT – INTELLIGENCE DIVISION.'*"

"That's the big time," Dick Dick said as he stroked his face with his hand. "Intelligence Division – that's the CIA. This is the big time, Lenny my friend."

"But that's still not the good part," Lenny said. "On another page he listed the budget for the project – nine hundred million."

"As in dollars?" Dick Dick asked.

"Nine hundred million dollars, and twenty-two million of that was allocated for acquiring and grading a building site."

"Damn," Dick Dick said. "I quoted him twenty million for Punky's land. I'd hate to leave two million lying on the table."

"It would look suspicious if we quoted the same exact amount that he had budgeted, don't you think?" Lenny asked.

"I suppose," Dick Dick said, "but I'd sure like to have that extra two million."

"There's more," Lenny said. "I saw his agenda. After he leaves Okoboji Gatlin's going to Hutchinson, Kansas and Pueblo, Colorado. Those must be the two building sites that he's considering."

"Did his agenda say when he was leaving?" Dick Dick asked.

"Just like he told us, he's leaving on Monday or Tuesday," Lenny said.

"Good job," Dick Dick said. "I have some thinking to do. I'll meet you at the Barefoot Bar at five thirty."

"Going for a boat ride?" Lenny asked.

"An hour on the water and I'll have it all figured out," Dick Dick said.

"Well, here's one to sharpen your saw with," Lenny said. "What number of each type of animal did Moses take on the ark?"

"That's an easy one," Dick Dick said. "Moses didn't have an ark."

"Very astute, Mr. Two Dicks," Lenny said.

"It was John the Baptist who had the ark," Dick Dick said with a smile.

Chapter
11

Gat stopped at Bob's Drive-In along the shore of West Lake Okoboji and placed an order for a "Bob Dog," onion rings, and soda.

"Welcome to Bob's," the cook yelled to him from the kitchen a few feet behind the order counter as he prepared Gat's order. "When did you get into town?"

"I got into town yesterday," Gat answered. "My first visit to Okoboji."

"So how do you like our little resort area?" the cook asked as he came around the counter to shake hands.

"It's unique – and beautiful," Gat said.

"I'm Myles," he said, "and you're the guy from Rhode Island, Gatlin."

"That's right," Gat said with a smile, "how did you know?"

"It's a small town and word travels fast – and besides that, I was sitting at the bar in Ruebins last night when you and Zach came in the back door."

"I've had a wonderful time here so far," Gat said. "Last night I hit a half dozen night spots and today a real estate agent gave me a tour of the area – and he didn't even try to sell me a house!"

"Obviously he's up to something; watch him," Myles joked.

A friend of Gatlin's has a favorite saying, "Most things said in jest are true." In this case, Gat believed that the off-hand comment made by Myles had more than a little truth in it.

Myles turned to go back to the kitchen.

"I have a question for you," Gat said.

"Yes," Myles said.

"Aren't you going to ask me a riddle? Everybody I've met has thrown one at me."

"Here's a legal question for you. Even though you're not from Iowa, you realize that the state of Iowa imposes upon you the duty to know and follow its laws, and that you're bound by those laws, right?" Myles said.

"Yes, I realize that," Gat said.

"Well then, here's the question: In the state of Iowa, is it permissible for a man to marry his widow's sister?"

Gat thought for a moment and then his face broke into a thin smile. "If his wife's a widow, then he's . . . ."

"You've got it," Myles said with a smile. "Enjoy your meal."

The view from the outdoor patio was spectacular, over-looking the volleyball players and sunbathers on the beach and providing a view of dozens of boats motoring across the lake.

Gat finished his meal and walked slowly along the lake toward the pier where he had gone for a break from the Rock the Roof concert the night before. Numerous tourists wandered around the pier, enjoying the view or reading the bronze plaques that provided information about formation of the lakes by the glaciers or about the fundraiser to save the amusement park from sale to a developer several years before.

Gat stopped at the Nutty Bar stand for the perfect desert after his Bob Dog. He leisurely browsed through the Queen's Court shops on the way to his primary destination, the Iowa Welcome Center.

The Iowa Welcome Center is housed in a bright yellow building a half block from the Arnolds Park Amusement Park. Gat walked in and was immediately greeted as soon as he crossed the threshold. "I'm Beryl," she said. "Welcome to the Iowa Great Lakes. Please sign our guest register. We have free maps of the Iowa Great Lakes and of the state of Iowa, free discount coupons, and lots of other information in those display racks over there."

"Thank you," Gat said as he signed the guest register.

"We get visitors from every state in the U.S. and from quite a few foreign countries, but we don't get too many people from Rhode Island," Beryl said. "Welcome to the state of Iowa."

"There's only about a million people in the whole state, so even if all of us were out traveling around America, we'd be spread pretty thin," Gat said.

"Mary, Jim," Beryl said as she waved at a couple who were straightening brochures to join them.

"This is Mary and Jim Quitno," Beryl said. "They are my super volunteers who help me out a couple of days a week. I'd be sunk without them. And this gentleman," she said gesturing to Gat, "is from Rhode Island."

"Gatlin Guthrie," Gat said as he shook hands with both of them.

"We took a drive along the east coast a few years ago and spent two nights in Providence," Jim said. "We both agreed that it's one of the most beautiful cities we've ever been in. That's an unusual name, Gatlin, at least for around here."

"But it's a very solid name, very strong," Mary said.

"My friends simply call me Gat," he replied.

"Lots of people have abbreviated names or nicknames," Beryl said with a smile. "For instance, I have a nickname for Jim."

Mary and Beryl broke into laughter. Jim pointed his finger at Beryl and said, "Beryl, don't you dare."

"I have a cute nickname for him but he doesn't want anyone to know it," Beryl said.

"Beryl, I'll quit on the spot; my volunteering days will be over," he threatened.

"Will you put that in writing?" Beryl teased.

Everybody likes to get in on a secret and likes to know something that not everyone knows. By now, a half dozen people had gathered 'round, waiting to find out this guy's secret nickname.

Jim glanced at the crowd that continued to grow and repeated himself, "Don't you dare."

Beryl ignored him and said, "Jim Quitno's secret nickname is . . ."

Several people in the crowd, which had grown to a dozen by now, leaned closer to make sure they didn't miss it.

"His nickname is . . ." Beryl paused and motioned for Gat to move closer. She leaned toward him and whispered the nickname in his ear so no one else could hear.

Gat broke into a wide smile. "That's a great nickname," he said, "and I agree, it's *cute*."

Mary and Beryl laughed as Jim rolled his eyes before he, too, broke into laughter.

"Looks like you folks have a good time here in the Welcome Center," Gat said.

"We're here because we want to be," Mary said. "It's a fun place to spend a couple of days a week and we meet lots of interesting people."

Gat wandered through the Welcome Center, browsing through some of the brochures, looking at maps of the area, admiring the products with an Iowa or Okoboji theme that were for sale, and just enjoying being a tourist.

"I've been a friend of Jim's for twenty-five years and didn't even know he had a nickname," a guy said to Gat in a hushed tone. "Would you tell me what it is – I'd like to get something on him that I can use."

"I'm new in town and don't want to start any rumors or riots or anything," Gat said with a smile, "so I'd better not.

But now that you know he's got a nickname, you can work him over until he caves in and tells you."

"Exactly what I was thinking," the man said with a smile. "Enjoy your visit to Okoboji."

The Iowa Welcome Center is home of the Maritime Museum that has a variety of nautical items on display including boats that sunk many years ago and that were found by divers. Instead of trying to sell the sunken treasures, the finders had donated them to the Museum so that everyone could enjoy them. It was, simply, the Okoboji way of doing things.

After enjoying the displays in the Welcome Center and Museum, Gat walked next door to the Iowa Great Lakes Chamber of Commerce, which is also housed in the big yellow building.

"Do you have any information on the available labor force in this area?" Gat asked.

"Hi, I'm Stacy," she said as she grabbed a brochure and handed it to Gat. "Are you familiar with the Iowa Great Lakes Corridor of Opportunity?"

"No, I'm not," Gat replied.

"Well," Stacy said, "the Iowa Great Lakes Corridor of Opportunity is an association of all the communities in Buena Vista, Clay, Dickinson, and Emmet counties. We all work together to provide existing and potential businesses with all of the assistance that we can to help them become and to remain successful."

Gat browsed through the brochure as she continued describing the virtues of the area.

"This brochure contains exactly what I was looking for," Gat said.

"Our motto is *Live, Work, Play Here*," Stacy said. "You'll never find better people or harder workers than we have here in the Corridor of Opportunity and you'll never find a better quality of life than we have here in the Iowa Great Lakes area. Are you thinking of starting a business here or moving one here?"

"I'm just a tourist passing through," Gat replied, "but I can see that the area has a lot to offer."

"By the way," Gat said, "are you the ones running the Great Treasure Hunt promotion?"

"Yes we are," she replied proudly. "If you're going to ask me for the next clue, I'll have to tell you the same thing that I told the other two hundred people who asked me for it today – sorry, no can do."

"I was just going to compliment you on such a successful promotion," Gat said. "Everywhere I go everyone is asking each other riddles and talking about the clues, and really getting involved – the sign of a great promotion."

"And, we don't let anyone leave our office without giving them the *Riddle of the Day*. Are you up for it?" Stacy asked.

"I have a feeling you're going to ask me anyway, so let's hear it," Gat said.

"Okay," Stacy said, "the *Riddle of the Day* – What gets wetter the more that it dries?"

"I would say that would be a towel," Gat answered.

"Good job!" she replied as she placed a mark under the "Correct" heading on her tally sheet. "So far today, we've had 376 correct answers and 89 incorrect ones. We try to keep the *Riddle of the Day* pretty basic so people at least have a fighting chance of getting it correct."

"I'm sure I'll be dreaming about riddles for the next two weeks," Gat said with a smile as he turned toward the door.

"If we can help in any way or if we can provide more information, please let us know," Stacy said. "And enjoy your Okoboji visit."

Chapter

12

The Barefoot Bar is located at Parks Marina on East Lake Okoboji a couple of miles east of the town of Okoboji.

It is an outdoor area with a casual flavor with the bars, gift shop, and restrooms designed as tiki huts.

The Barefoot Bar is Okoboji's largest bar and on a hot sunny day, more than 1,500 partiers sit at tables under large umbrellas, gather at one of the tiki bars, or simply wander around with drink in hand to see who they might know or might want to know.

The Barefoot Bar can be reached by either land or water and there is a large dock system that can accommodate hundreds of boats. On any day of the week, anything from jet skis to cabin cruisers worth hundreds of thousands of dollars are tied up at the dock.

On this particular Friday evening, the sun was hot, there was a gentle breeze, the calm waters of East Lake Okoboji were glistening, and the Barefoot Bar was alive. And, there is no better place to meet your riddle-solving teammates to listen to the new clue to the Great Okoboji Treasure Hunt. If you couldn't solve the riddle, you could at least throw down a few cool ones and forget about it until the new clue on Saturday morning.

Lenny had arrived at the Barefoot Bar early and had commandeered a table as close to the lake and as far away as he could from any other tables or the stage where the band would be playing later on. Since the table was on the edge of the seating area, it provided a view of the entire Barefoot Bar where he and the other Wise Men could keep an eye out for Gatlin, Punky, or anyone else who might mess up their plans.

Dick Dick arrived at five thirty and Sleepy came lumbering in a few minutes later.

"This is a great place to have a drink and to watch women in bikinis," Dick Dick said, "but for carrying on a private conversation, it's like a cornfield – too many ears. So, after the clue is given, and we listen to a couple of songs from the band, let's meet back at my office to plan our next step."

Harley Rides, one of the many private taxi services in the lakes area, that gets ninety-nine percent of its business from the bar trade, delivered Gat to the Barefoot Bar. A ten dollar fare and a five dollar tip was worth not having to fight the traffic, jockeying for a parking place, and maybe running afoul of the law for driving after having a cocktail or two.

Gat stood at the edge of the Barefoot Bar and surveyed the scene. If someone had blindfolded him, led him to this spot, ripped off the blindfold, and asked him where he was, he would have had trouble deciding if he was in Key West or Key Largo, or maybe the Flora-Bama bar.

Gat ordered a margarita from a bartender wearing an Iowa Hawkeye shirt and a Hawkeye cap. "I'm new in town," Gat said, "but I bet I know who you are – you're the Number One Iowa Hawkeye Fan of Okoboji – I read about you in the *Okoboji* novel."

"Brian Reynolds," he answered with a grin. "The Hawkeyes will go at least ten and two and maybe even eleven and one this year in football. I predict a top ten finish and a New Year's Day bowl game. And remember, you heard it here first."

"Are you always right with your predictions?" Gat asked.

"Hardly ever," Brian answered with a smile, "but when I am, I make sure nobody forgets it. Well, you know who I am, but who are you?"

"Gatlin Guthrie from Rhode Island, just passing through on my way to Kansas and Colorado. You can call me Gat if you like."

"Gat, welcome to the Barefoot Bar. I'm the manager and if you need anything, let me know. Stick around – the reading of the new clue in the Treasure Hunt is at six and we've got a great band, Richie Lee, starting right after that."

"Oh, Oh," Lenny said, nodding to where Gat and Brian were shaking hands. "How the hell did he get out here?"

"No problem," Dick Dick said. "It doesn't matter who he talks to as long as it's not Punky, and Punky never comes out here – too many people for him to be the center of attention with his theories and philosophies. I'm going to go ask our new friend, Gatlin, to join us. That way we can be sure he doesn't talk to anybody we don't want him to."

Dick Dick was about to rise from his chair when he spotted Gatlin visiting with a young woman, talking and laughing like they were old friends. "Who's that he's talking to?" he asked Sleepy and Lenny.

"That's Stacy from the Chamber office," Lenny said.

"How in the hell would he know her?" Dick Dick asked.

"I don't know but I'll find out just as soon as he moves along," Lenny said.

The Three Wise men watched Gat as he moved through the crowd, stopping to visit with Deano and Jody, Zach, Doris and her group from the Rock 'N Roll Museum, Maestro Horsman, Myles and his wife from Bob's Drive-In, and several others.

"He's been in town for two days and he knows more people than I do," Sleepy said.

"I've been watching his body language carefully when he's talking with all of those people," Lenny said. "It's just casual, lighthearted social conversation – nothing serious or business-related at all. When I competed in debate competitions, I learned that a person's body language often speaks louder than their words and I've found this to be true of witnesses and jurors in court also. He's just having a good time. He doesn't suspect a thing."

"I found the same thing about body language to be true in sales," Dick Dick said. "I have a saying, 'All buyers are liars,' but if you forget about the words they say and you look in their eyes and watch their body language, you can learn the truth."

"Amen, brother," Sleepy said.

Stacy from the Chamber of Commerce office was standing by the tiki hut bar when Lenny approached her. "Hey, Stace," he said as he raised his glass to toast hers, "isn't it great to be in Okoboji!"

"If you're going to ask me what the new clue is, don't, because I don't know what it is myself. I have to wait until it is announced, just like everyone else," she said.

"No, No," Lenny said, "I wasn't going to ask you about the clue. But, I was going to ask you who that tall guy with silver hair was that you were talking to a moment ago – he looks familiar."

"He stopped by the Chamber office for some information earlier today. That's about all I know about him," She said.

"What kind of information?" Lenny asked.

"Oh, just some brochures about the area – the normal stuff we hand out by the thousands every year," Stacy said, sensing that Lenny was getting a little too curious.

"I think he's from back east – maybe Rhode Island," Lenny said, hoping to lead Stacy into revealing some additional information about Gatlin's mission at the Chamber office.

"Could be. I really don't know. But, he's a nice guy and if you're curious, why don't you ask him? He's right over there," Stacy said pointing toward the middle of the crowd.

"I'll do that," Lenny said. "Have a nice weekend."

Lenny turned to search for Gatlin and he almost fell through the cement patio. There, coming straight toward Gatlin, was Punky Cox. That damned Punky Cox. There was no way that he could rush up to one of them or the other to intervene or to steer them away from each other. There was nothing that he could do but to let it play out. And to observe the body language as they came closer and closer to each other and finally passed within three feet of one another.

Gatlin and Punky didn't flinch; they didn't make eye contact; they didn't even notice one another. It was just another person that they met in that steady stream of strangers wandering through the tables at the Barefoot Bar.

The Barefoot Bar was filling up fast and people were grabbing tables and chairs as fast as bar manager Brian could haul them out of storage. He placed a table directly in front of the stage and motioned to Gat that he should sit there. "We always have a special table, front and center, for our guests from Rhode Island," Brian said.

Lenny kept an eye on Gatlin and as soon as he sat down at the table that Brian had provided, Lenny headed straight for Punky.

"We missed you last night at The Gardens," Lenny said.

"I had a touch of the flu," Punky answered, "but I'm

feeling better now – great, in fact. Sleepy and I went up to Jackpot Junction today and I hit five out of six on Keno seven times, but I just couldn't get over the hump and hit the big one."

"Come over and join Dick Dick, Sleepy, and me – we've got a table with a view of the lake and of all the action at the bar."

"I normally don't come out here – too many people to carry on a good conversation, but everybody says it's a great place to listen to the Friday night clue, so I thought I'd check it out," Punky said. "I'm going to the Wine Bar right after the clue is revealed. George Stewart is reading some of his poetry and then we'll sit around and drink wine and discuss his words. It's really a good time; you should join us sometime."

"Sounds like a blast," Lenny said dryly.

"Attention everyone, attention," a pretty young woman with long dark hair said over the public address system from the stage. "Attention."

"I'm Debbie, and welcome to Friday night at the Barefoot Bar. In just a minute we'll turn on KUOO radio for the Friday night clue to the Great Okoboji Treasure Hunt."

Applause. Clapping. Whistling.

"After the reading of the clue, Richie Lee and an Okoboji all-star band will be taking the stage to play some of your favorite songs. So, hang around, have a drink, have a good time, and good luck in solving the riddle for this week's Treasure Hunt."

"Hello, everyone," the voice coming over the speakers

said. "This is Mary Treanor from KUOO Radio and it is my pleasure to bring you the second clue to this week's Great Okoboji Treasure Hunt. Two armed police officers, Stacy Schomaker and Jason Petersen, are standing beside me holding a locked strongbox that contains tonight's clue. But first, for a little practice, I have a riddle for you. After I read it, call me at 712-336-KUOO - that's 712-336-5866. The first person that calls in with the correct answer will get a free dinner for two at Mineral City restaurant in Arnolds Park.

"Now here is tonight's warm-up riddle: 'What is the longest word that can be typed using only the top alphabet row of a keyboard?' The phone lines are open, call me at 712-336-KUOO."

The phones rang immediately. Doug, calling from the Dry Dock deck guessed "Write." Shelly called from Captain's Getaway with "Porter." Albert called from his hospital bed with "Pity." Kelsey called from Ruebins with "Try." Joyce called from the Barefoot Bar with "Typewriter."

"That's right!" Mary Treanor said, and the Barefoot Bar crowd burst into applause as Joyce walked to the stage to take a bow.

"Well, now it's time for the Friday night clue to the Great Okoboji Treasure Hunt," Mary said. "But first, as a reminder, here is a repeat of the first clue that was revealed at the Rock the Roof concert last night: Clue Number One was: 'Sometimes our best plans fall, because we simply think too small. And that could be true of me – me in all my majesty.'

"The police officers are placing the strongbox on the

desk in front of me and now Stacy is handing me the key to the padlock. I have now unlocked the padlock and am now removing a sealed envelope with the words, Great Okoboji Treasure Hunt, Clue Number Two. I am now opening the envelope and removing the clue, and here it is. Here is Clue Number Two to this week's riddle for the Great Okoboji Treasure Hunt: 'You've seen me a time or three, but probably paid me very little heed. Every day you depend on me; I've got what you want and what you need.'"

Mary read the clue a second time, slowly, so everyone could copy it, and then she read it a third time, just to make sure that everyone had it down correctly. "And that's it for the Friday night clue and we now return to our regular programming – this is Mary Treanor and you're listening to Campus Radio, KUOO."

Riddle solving teams discussed the latest clue and even those who weren't planning to participate in the Treasure Hunt threw out ideas for others to digest. It was almost a consensus among the partiers at the Barefoot Bar that the words, "I've got what you want and what you need," obviously referred to booze and the clue was undoubtedly hidden in some liquor store. But, which one? Oh well, let's have another drink and we'll figure it out in the morning after the ten o'clock clue.

Immediately after the clue was read, Punky jumped up from the table and bid Dick Dick, Lenny, and Sleepy farewell saying, "I'll see you Thursday afternoon at The Gardens, or maybe at the *Hungover and Broke* gathering at the Dry Dock

Sunday morning." He tore through the crowd at a near trot. Perhaps Punky was in a hurry to distance himself from this crowd of beer and whiskey guzzlers and to join the sippers at the Wine Bar. Perhaps he wanted to give everyone the impression that this sophisticated, professorial-looking gentleman with the wire-rimmed glasses and driving cap had solved the riddle and was rushing out to claim the treasure. Perhaps he just wanted to get the hell out of there for reasons unknown to anyone, including himself.

Whatever the reason, Punky was leaving the Barefoot Bar at a brisk clip and The Three Wise Men were glad to see him go. He had not met Gatlin Guthrie and didn't even know that he existed and that was exactly the way The Three Wise Men intended to keep it for the next two or three days.

Richie Lee is a young man in his early twenties who started playing guitar and singing on stage when he was twelve years old. He was an unusual youth in that he took little pleasure in the music of his own generation, preferring instead the songs from an era some thirty years before he was born. Even at age twelve, he took the stage wearing a suit with his hair combed back, strapped on his guitar, pulled a pair of black rimmed glasses from his pocket, put them on, and tore into a medley of songs by Buddy Holly and Ritchie Valens.

Now, nearly a decade after he began performing on stage, Richie Lee was a seasoned professional. His hair is still slicked back like the rockers of the late fifties and early sixties, but he has traded in his suit for black slacks and flowing silk shirts. His repertoire consists of classic rock songs from the late fifties and the sixties and he knows every song ever sung by Buddy Holly and Ritchie Valens. And, Richie Lee doesn't just embrace this era and its music; he lives it.

When Richie plays gigs near his home in Des Moines, he uses the same group of musicians as his backup band. When he travels out of the area, as when he performs in Okoboji, he often uses local musicians. Tonight at the Barefoot Bar his backup band consisted of Steve Streit and Christopher Jon on guitar, Al Klein on drums, Denny Kintzi on keyboards, and Shane Von Holdt on bass.

Richie Lee and the band tore into one Buddy Holly song after another including "Maybe Baby," "Rave On," "Peggy Sue," and "That'll Be The Day." Dancers crowded the dance area from the first bar of the first song and didn't leave until Richie announced, "In the tradition of the Great Okoboji Treasure Hunt, I have a riddle for you, and whoever gets it right will receive a free round of drinks for their entire table compliments of the Barefoot Bar."

Now that was a prize that this bunch could appreciate and that was worth fighting for. The jabbering and chatting stopped as everyone listened intently for Richie's riddle.

"What is it about the song 'Unchained Melody,' made famous by the Righteous Brothers, that is extremely unique?" Richie said.

Just in case that some people didn't recognize the title, Richie and the band launched into the first few words of the song, "Oh, my love, my darling, I've hungered . . . ."

"If you have an answer to this riddle, come up here and

say it into the microphone, so everyone can hear it," Richie said.

In a flash, there was a mad dash of would-be riddle solvers heading for the stage in an attempt to claim the coveted prize. Each took their turn at the microphone and each was sent packing without the prize, "It is a song that has such high notes that it is impossible for normal humans to sing," "It was originally America's national anthem," "It has been recorded more than any other song in history," "Only four people on earth know the correct words to the song," "The melody was originally intended to be a Christmas song," "It has exactly two hundred words in it," "The unique thing about the song is that there is nothing unique about it," "It was written by a bunch of prisoners on the chain gang," "The song was named after a racehorse," "The song was written about a wild woman named Melody," "The song was written about a woman named Melody who was released from the chain gang," "The song was originally locked up in a box and somebody had to cut the chains to release the melody."

Each response was met with cheers, jeers, laughter, whistles, shouts of approval, or boos. Finally, after the final entry, Richie revealed the correct answer, "In virtually every song ever written, the title is repeated from maybe four to ten times within the song. In the song "Unchained Melody," the unique thing is that the title is not mentioned even once in the song."

About a hundred voices said in unison, "No shit."

One of the guys in the band yelled to the bar manager,

"Brian, the band claims the round of drinks for stumping the crowd."

Brian smiled and shouted to his bar staff, "Give the band a round on Butch Parks."

The band raised their drinks high in a toast to the crowd and the crowd responded in kind, raising their glasses to salute the band. "Let's have a swaller and a holler," Kintzi shouted and a thousand swigs were thrown down, followed by shouts of "Hee Haw," "Yee Haw," "Hell Yah," "Sooey," and the like.

The band launched into Ritchie Valens' "La Bamba," which got the dance crowd back in action.

They were standing in the back, totally unnoticed by the crowd that was focused on the band and on the "Unchained Melody" riddle.

"I don't see him anywhere," the blonde said.

"We've looked everywhere all day long," the redhead replied. "I can't believe he would just up and leave without doing what he came here to do."

Four people got up from their table near the front and headed for the dance area.

The redhead craned her neck to peer through the opening where the people had sat. "That's *Him!*" she said. "That's *Him.*"

The blonde looked where the redhead was pointing and agreed, "It is. It's *Him.*"

"It makes sense that he would be given the best seat in the house, front and center," the redhead said.

"Who else but *Him* would deserve it!" the blonde said.

"We can't lose him again without making our move," the redhead said.

"That's why we came here," the blonde said. "Let's do it."

They skirted the crowd virtually unnoticed until they were at the front of the crowd but off to the side, where they were still unnoticed.

They were dressed in identical outfits to what they wore the night before except that they were in different colors. The blonde wore a tight red dress that came six inches above her knees and that hugged every voluptuous curve of her body. Last night the redhead had worn a black leather outfit; tonight it was white, consisting of a leather bustier, skimpy leather shorts, and knee-high boots with stiletto heels.

As soon as the last notes of "La Bamba" faded away, the two made their move, walking in front of the crowd toward Gat's table. But, they didn't walk, they strutted their stuff, va-voom, va-voom, va-voom, va-voom.

A hush fell over the crowd. Some women have been known to be so dazzling that they could stop traffic. A few can even stop a train, but these two could stop a river.

Men's eyes popped open and their chins dropped to their belly buttons while their wives and girlfriends shot daggers at the blonde and the redhead. It has long been known that men are fascinated by promiscuous women, as long as it isn't their mother, sister, wife, or daughter. Women, on the other hand, would love to kill them regardless of who they might be, since any woman who looks like that and acts like that has got to be considered a potential rival. Her man may not be much, but dammit, he was hers and no floozy had better try to take him away.

They continued on, va-voom, va-voom, va-voom until they were directly in front of the stage. They turned in unison and walked straight for Gat's table. Bar manager Brian was carrying chairs that were intended for a table in the back, but he changed direction just in time to set them at Gat's table for the two bombshells.

The band hadn't played a note, or even thought of doing so for the past thirty seconds, as they watched in awe as the spectacle unfolded in front of them. Each of them had been upstaged before in their musical careers, but never like this. Finally realizing that they might not be able to muster the proper concentration to play a song, Richie Lee said, "Let's take a little break."

"We know who you are," the blonde said to Gat.

"And we know why you're here," the redhead said.

"And we want in on it," the blonde said.

Gat stroked his chin to demonstrate that he was puzzled. "I don't understand," he said.

"Oh yes you do," the blonde said coyly, "but we know you've got to keep it quiet until you're ready to make your move."

"We've been watching you and we know a real pro when we see one," the redhead said. "We're professionals, too."

"That's why we want to work with you," the blonde added. "A group of professionals working together."

"Just exactly what are you professionals at?" Gat asked. From their appearance, two or three possibilities easily came to mind.

"You know," the blonde said with a wink.

"Same profession as you," the redhead whispered to Gat, as she nudged him gently with her elbow.

"We know you've got to keep a low profile and we don't want to blow your cover," the blonde said. "Why don't we go somewhere where we can talk in private."

"Well, you certainly have aroused my, uh, curiosity," Gat said. "Where do you want to go to have our little chat?"

"Our car is parked along the road; let's take a drive," the redhead said.

They rose from the table and the blonde attached herself to Gat's left arm while the redhead took his right one. Every eye in the place was on them as they slowly made their exit.

One man summed up the thoughts of every man in the place when he blurted out, "That lucky dog," which was followed, predictably, by a sharp elbow in the ribs from his wife.

The Three Wise Men had watched it all in shocked silence. "What in the hell is going on?" Dick Dick said.

"I think it's safe to say those two aren't interested in defense contracts," Lenny said. "In fact, I'd guess they're probably better at offense than at defense."

"I guess it won't hurt anything if he has a little fun while he's in Okoboji," Dick Dick said. "At least we know he'll be occupied for the evening and I doubt the two of them will be taking Gatlin to the Wine Bar to sip wine with Punky."

"I've never even talked to that much woman in my whole life and he's got two of them shamelessly throwing themselves at him," Sleepy said. "What's he got that I ain't got?"

"For one thing, look in the mirror," Dick Dick said sarcastically. "And for another, even though your grandpa left you tens of millions, this guy's got hundreds of millions. Need any other reasons?"

"You don't have to say stuff like that," Sleepy said.

"Sorry that the truth hurts," Dick Dick said. "But remember, the truth will set you free."

"Who's the idiot that ever came up with that idea?" Sleepy said.

"I think it was Punky Cox," Lenny said.

"Enough of this bullshit," Dick Dick said. "Let's meet at my office in an hour and we'll put the final touches on our game plan."

Chapter

13

The blonde and the redhead led Gat to a fully restored, mint condition bright red 1964 Cadillac convertible. This was the golden era of automobiles before bucket seats, where a guys' girl could snuggle up to him or maybe even sit on his lap when he was driving. The blonde got behind the wheel, Gat got in the middle, and the redhead sat on the outside. If there had been another person, they could have fit them into the front seat also - another advantage of bench seats.

The blonde steered the Caddy onto Stakeout Road and headed toward Okoboji.

"Have you gotten into the riddles everybody's trying to solve here in Okoboji?" the redhead asked, making small talk to kill some time until they got down to business.

"At first I thought it was kind of corny, but everybody's been having so much fun with it that I've gotten swept up in it a little bit myself," Gat said.

"Well, here's one for you," the blonde said. "There are three women driving down the road sitting in the front seat of a pickup truck all dressed alike in cowgirl hats, denim shirts, jeans, and cowgirl boots. Which one is the real cowgirl?"

"I don't think there's any way to tell unless you give me more information," Gat said.

"The real cowgirl is the one in the middle," the blonde said. "First of all, she doesn't have to drive . . ."

"And, second, she doesn't have to open the gate," the redhead added.

The blonde pulled the car into the Higgins Museum parking lot and parked behind the building out of sight of any traffic passing on Lakeshore Drive. The Higgins Museum is a museum of money, much of which is old paper money issued by individual Iowa banks back in the days when this was a common practice. Even when the museum is open for visitors, a day or two might pass without a single footstep crossing the threshold. So now, after hours, this would be one of the quietest places on earth to have an uninterrupted meeting.

"I'm curious," Gat said. "What are you two up to?"

"We know who you are and we know why you're in Okoboji," the blonde said.

"And, we want to be a part of it," the redhead said.

"And just what is it that you think I'm up to?" Gat asked.

"We know you're from New York City, we know you're a movie producer, and we know you're going to make a movie here in Okoboji," the redhead said.

"And we want to be in your movie," the blonde said.

"Where did you hear about the movie?" Gat asked.

"We were in a bar in Omaha Tuesday night and this guy we met, Ken Horner, was telling us all about it - about how it's going to be an erotic movie and about how people from the area could audition to be in the movie," the blonde said.

"So we jumped in the car and got up here Wednesday afternoon. We hit every bar and restaurant and coffee house in Okoboji looking for you," the redhead said.

"And then when we saw you in The Gardens yesterday afternoon we knew it was you, and we've been observing you ever since, trying to learn all that we can," the blonde said.

"So your being in some of the same places that I was last night like Pirate Jack's and the Rock the Roof concert and Ruebins wasn't a coincidence?" Gat said.

"We weren't stalking you," the redhead said. "We were watching you, trying to learn all that we could about how you approached your craft of making a movie."

"But we couldn't keep up with you in these heels when you left Captain's and we lost you last night," the blonde said. "We were afraid that you had left Okoboji to go back to New York, so when we saw you tonight, we decided to audition for you right on the spot before we lost you again."

"Did you notice how we held the crowd at the Barefoot Bar in the palm of our hands?" the redhead asked.

"Did you see how some of the people were absolutely speechless by our entrance?" the blonde asked.

"We would be perfect for your erotic movie," the redhead said.

"Right," the blonde agreed. "We can be as erotic as you want, for the camera, of course."

Gat looked them over, sitting there in their tight-fitting, sexy clothes. "You dressed like this for me? For my erotic movie?"

"Just for you, just for our audition," the blonde said.

Gat broke into a smile and then began to laugh. It was one of those private laughs, like he knew something that was hilarious but that nobody else did.

"Wait a minute," the redhead said. "If there's two more erotic women in Okoboji, we'd like to see them."

"I'm not laughing at the two of you, believe me," Gat said. "And I'll bet there aren't two more erotic women in the whole state of Iowa."

"What's so funny, then?" the blonde asked.

"I think your friend, Horner, who told you about the movie got things confused a little bit," Gat said. "First of all, there is a movie that is being shot in Okoboji, but it's not an erotic movie; it's a documentary about exotic plants found on native prairie ground."

"What?" the blonde and redhead screamed in unison.

"There's more," Gat said. "I'm flattered that you would think I might be a movie producer and I appreciate all of your efforts to impress me with your audition, but I'm not a movie producer and I'm not from New York City. I'm a businessman from Rhode Island just passing through Okoboji on my way to Kansas and Colorado."

"You're just testing us, to see how we would react, right?"

the redhead asked hopefully.

"I wish that were true," Gat said, "but I'm giving it to you straight – I'm not from New York City and I'm not a movie producer."

The blonde and the redhead slumped down in the car seat and bowed their heads in shame. "We made fools of ourselves, didn't we," the redhead said as a matter of fact.

"And embarrassed ourselves in front of the whole town of Okoboji," the blonde said.

"At least they'll never know that it was us," the redhead said as she grabbed a handful of red hair and yanked off her wig, revealing a head of short auburn hair.

"Right," the blonde said as she pulled off the blonde wig and shook loose her coal black hair.

"It's probably just as well," the former redhead said. "We'd have never gone through with doing that erotic stuff anyway and besides, this leather outfit is hotter than hell and makes me sweat in places that I don't want to sweat."

"Well, there goes our fantasy of being in the movies, but it was fun pretending for a couple of days," the former blonde said.

"Don't give up your dream of being in the movies so easily," Gat said. "Remember that I said a documentary is going to be filmed about exotic plants? Well, the reason I know that is because I stopped at the Arnolds Park Library today, and I met the movie producer – the real movie producer. His name is Watts. He was there doing research, looking at maps of native prairie ground. We had a nice visit and he told me that he's going to hire two young men, or two young women – he'd prefer women, to feature in his documentary. The two of you would be perfect."

"You know," the former blonde said, "we'd actually fit into an exotic documentary better than an erotic movie anyway."

"You see, we're not exactly what we appeared to be tonight," the former redhead said. "In real life, she's a Professor of Sociology at the University of Nebraska and I'm a chiropractor. If we'd have gotten parts in an erotic movie we might have made more money than being in a documentary, but it would have probably ruined our careers."

"The movie producer is from New York City, by the way," Gat said, "and he's creating this documentary for National Public Television. He said it will be shown at least once a year on every public television station in all fifty states for the next ten years."

"Where can we find this guy, Watson?" the former blonde asked, suddenly being more than a little bit interested.

"The name's Watts, and he'll be at the Arnolds Park Public Library all day tomorrow. Just ask the librarian, Sue, to point him out and take it from there."

"Know what," the former redhead said, "our audition for you was a tremendous success after all. Without meeting you we would never have known about this documentary."

"And I would never have had the pleasure of meeting the two of you," Gat said.

"We're going to get out of these ridiculous outfits and slip into some jeans and T-shirts and hit some of the bars, without our wigs, of course," the former blonde said. "Want to go along?"

"Why don't you just drop me at the Four Seasons Resort, and maybe I'll bump into you later on," Gat said.

The two of them put their wigs back on, to stay in character, until they could slip into their motel room and bid the blonde and the redhead goodbye forever.

They dropped Gat off at the Four Seasons and he watched them drive away, hoping that one day he would see them again, on National Public Television.

Chapter
14

The Three Wise Men were seated at a finely crafted solid oak table in the conference room at Dick Dick Realty.

During those times when Dick Dick was rich, he believed in conspicuous consumption, buying the finest trappings that money could buy. When it came to business, Dick Dick's motto was, "Look prosperous – people want to deal with someone who appears to be successful because they think it will rub off on them." When it came to his personal life, when he was rich, his motto was, "If you've got it, flaunt it." During times when he was flat broke, Dick Dick's philosophy was simple, "Don't let 'em see you sweat."

Even though Dick Dick had been broke twice, he was rich now, and in a few days, if all went well, he would be twice as rich.

"Lenny, bring Sleepy up to speed on what you found when you broke into Gatlin's motel room," Dick Dick said.

"For the record, I did not break into Gatlin Guthrie's motel room," Lenny said. "I simply went to visit a new friend to invite him to breakfast, found the door to his motel room ajar and, fearing that he might be ill or hurt, I entered the room to check on his safety. Instead of being accused of breaking into his room, I should be given a commendation for checking on his welfare."

"Spoken like a true lawyer," Dick Dick said, "but you're not in court here and Sleepy and I don't care how the hell you got into the room, I just want you to tell Sleepy what you told me about what you found."

Lenny had to smile to himself. Through the years he had honed his skills to the point where it didn't matter if he was representing the plaintiff for the defendant in a particular lawsuit, he could spin a story either way to fit the situation in support of his client's contention. Truth? The hell with it. He was out to win the case for his client and to collect his contingency fee, which had risen to a whopping forty percent of what his client won.

One of Lenny's most famous cases involved defending a wealthy contractor whose dog bit his teenage daughter's boyfriend in the face, which caused permanent scars and disfiguration.

The dog *allegedly* bit the teenage daughter's boyfriend.

Lenny's line of defense was simple: (1) The daughter doesn't have a boyfriend, (2) The contractor doesn't have a dog, (3) If the contractor had a dog, it wouldn't bite, (4) If the dog bit the boyfriend, it wouldn't bite him in the face, (5) If it bit him in the face, it wouldn't cause scars like those, (6) If it caused scars like those, they would heal by themselves in time and there would be no harm done.

And, the jury bought it.

Lenny didn't even have to resort to his final contention, his ace in the hole: (7) The contractor doesn't have a daughter.

"Long story short," Lenny said. "I found Gatlin's briefcase and opened it up. Inside was a blueprint of a layout consisting of a huge building of 150,000 square feet and several smaller buildings surrounding the big building. There was a series of fences and barricades surrounding the buildings and outside of the fences were parking lots. The heading on the blueprint said, *'CONFIDENTIAL – PROPERTY OF THE UNITED STATES GOVERNMENT DEFENSE DEPARTMENT – INTELLIGENCE DIVISION.'* "

"Whew," Sleepy whistled. "This is serious stuff. Intelligence Division – that's the CIA, isn't it?"

"Cloaks, daggers, spies, secret codes, wiretapping, guns that shoot around corners – the whole nine yards," Dick Dick said.

"A building measuring 150,000 square feet, that's huge. My house only has 14,000 square feet – the building's eleven or twelve times the size of my house!" Sleepy said.

"The main building is larger than three football fields," Dick Dick said. "And, we don't know how large the other buildings are, but they might add up to another hundred thousand or maybe even two hundred thousand square feet."

"Whew," Sleepy said.

"Lenny, tell him about the building site," Dick Dick

said in a voice full of excitement.

"There was a sheet that showed they planned on a thousand acres for the project," Lenny said.

"And Punky and his sister have 960 acres," Dick Dick said. "I would think that would be close enough – within forty acres of their projected site."

"And it just keeps getting better," Lenny said. "The sheet showed that they have budgeted nine hundred million for the project and that twenty-two million of that was for the building site, which includes site preparation."

"And Punky wants ten million, right?" Sleepy said.

"That's what he says," Dick Dick said, "but we'll offer him five million, which is still an awful lot for that piece of ground. When the money's on the table he might sing a different tune and take it."

"If we can turn around and sell the land to Gatlin for twenty million, that would be a profit of fifteen million to be split three ways – five million profit each," Lenny said.

"Even if we have to pay Punky the full ten million, we'll still net over three million each," Dick Dick said.

"Not bad for two or three days' work," Lenny said with a smile as he rubbed his hands together.

"What makes you think that Gatlin might even be interested in putting his CIA building here in Okoboji?" Sleepy asked.

"Remember what Stacy from the Chamber office told Lenny, that Gatlin came into the Chamber office looking for some information and she gave him some brochures to take with him to study," Dick Dick said.

"Yes, I remember," Sleepy said.

"Well, what kind of information does someone go to the Chamber of Commerce office for?" Dick Dick asked. He continued on, answering his own question. "Not for information about entertainment or the amusement park or motels or concerts or things to do in the area – all that is available at the Welcome Center next door to the Chamber office. No, a person goes to the Chamber of Commerce office to get information about business-related things, like the available labor pool in the area, industrial development sites, housing, utility rates – stuff like that."

"I see what you mean, but what if we buy the land from Punky and then Gatlin won't go through with the deal?" Sleepy asked.

"We'll make sure that Gatlin commits to it first," Dick Dick said. "It will require precision timing. First, I'll talk to Gatlin to see if I can sell him on the idea of putting his CIA building here in Okoboji. Then, I'll feel Punky out and tell him I've got somebody who is interested in his land and see what he says. Then, I'll work both ends against the middle and put the deal together."

"Sounds simple enough," Sleepy said.

"It's a routine real estate transaction like I handle every day, except the numbers are a little bigger," Dick Dick said. "It'll work. Trust me."

"Did you get the Land Trust set up today?" Sleepy asked Lenny.

"Got it done this afternoon," Lenny said. "The way it works is this – if it looks like the deal is going to go together, we each put our money into the Land Trust and the Land Trust buys Punky's land. The beauty of the Land Trust is that none of our names will appear on the deed or on any other public documents, so no one will know that it's actually us putting this deal together. Dick Dick won't reveal to Punky the names of the owners of the Land Trust, which is, of course, the three of us. In fact, legally, Dick Dick will be obligated to only tell Punky that the buyer is the Okoboji Beneficial Land Trust, which is the name I picked for our Land Trust. Likewise, Dick Dick will only reveal to Gatlin that the owner of the land that he's buying is the Okoboji Beneficial Land Trust."

"Sweet," Sleepy said.

"I took a little boat ride this afternoon and did some thinking," Dick Dick said. "The profit we make from flipping Punky's land is only the tip of the iceberg. A very small tip of a very large iceberg."

"How's that?" Sleepy asked.

"We don't know for sure what the total square feet is of all of the buildings in the project, but let's say that the total will be at least 250,000 square feet. That's office space larger than five football fields. How many people do you think it will take to fill up that much office space?" Dick Dick asked.

"Well, if each office was two hundred square feet, that would be more than a thousand people. If each office was a hundred square feet, that would be twenty-five hundred people, or maybe even more," Lenny said.

"And the CIA never sleeps, they'll man the offices 'round the clock," Dick Dick said, "so there could be three times that many people working there."

"And that doesn't include the security staff, grounds-keepers, janitorial staff, food service, and all that stuff," Sleepy said.

"Which all means that somewhere around, say, four, five, six, or even seven thousand workers will need to move into the Okoboji area, and at 2.7 people per household, on average, that's bringing in ten to fifteen thousand new residents," Dick Dick said.

"That will essentially double the permanent population of the lakes area," Lenny said.

"And these are well-paid federal government employees, so it will double the economy in the lakes area in a matter of three years," Dick Dick said.

"And we can capitalize on all of that growth," Lenny said.

"Right," Dick Dick said. "Since we will know that this is going to happen before anyone else in the whole area, we can buy up land for housing developments through our Land Trust, buy apartment buildings, maybe buy a lumber yard or two – the potential is unlimited."

"And that means, Sleepy, your banks will make millions on real estate loans, and Dick Dick your real estate company will become the largest agency the area has ever seen and you'll likewise make millions," Lenny said. "And as for me, well, a doubling of the population should result in quadrupling the number of lawsuits in the area – I can hardly wait."

"Besides all that," Sleepy said slowly, "the three of us will be local heroes. We will be the ones who created the greatest growth that this area has ever seen or will ever see. We will be the ones that others will point to when they talk about people of vision. We will be the ones that everyone in the community, if not the entire state, will look up to and admire and respect for pulling off one of the biggest coups in the state's history by bringing in a U.S. Defense Contract."

Sleepy already had money - his grandfather's money. What he didn't have was respect, since he had never accomplished anything on his own and everybody in the area was well aware of his various failed follies. But this would be his chance to show them all that he, Stephen Southworth, III, was a highly capable entrepreneur in his own right and was a force to be reckoned with. Yes, this was the project that would put Stephen Southworth, III on the map.

"By the way, Lenny," Dick Dick said, "that For Sale sign that you put up on Punky's land was perfect, very professional. I almost believed it myself."

"There's one other thing I did today," Lenny said. "I store real estate abstracts for hundreds of my clients in the fireproof vault in my office, including the abstracts for Punky's two pieces of land. I went to the courthouse and checked the color of title of Punky's land and found no encumbrances whatsoever – no mortgages, no judgments, nothing. Punky and his sister own it free and clear."

"How about the deed - both Punky and his sister will need to sign the deed and she's down in Alabama," Sleepy said.

"A couple of years ago, upon her request, I drafted a universal power of attorney giving Punky the power to handle any and all transactions on her behalf pertaining to the land. He can sign on her behalf and transfer good title without her even being here," Lenny explained.

Dick Dick smiled. "Things are falling into place beautifully."

"So, Dick Dick, when are you going to meet with Gatlin?" Sleepy asked.

"It sounds like everything is set and we've got everything ready to go, so I'm going to invite him for a boat ride tomorrow morning, after the ten o'clock clue is given," Dick Dick said. "There are three reasons for taking him out on the boat. First, the majesty of the lake will be a constant reminder to him of what a great area this is. Second, I do my best thinking out on the lake and I want to be mentally sharp. Third, he won't be able to get away from me unless he jumps overboard and swims to shore."

"There is one other matter that we need to take care of, and that's the money," Lenny said. "Assuming that we might need to pay the full price of ten million to buy Punky's land, we will each need to be ready to deposit 3.3333 million in cash into the Land Trust at a moment's notice."

"I already have mine in an account ready to be transferred," Sleepy said.

"As do I," Lenny said.

"My money's mostly tied up in hard assets – land, this office, vehicles, boats, stuff like that, and some mutual funds and stocks, and your bank's going to give me a short-term loan for my share, right Sleepy?" Dick Dick said.

"That's right, Dick Dick, but you've got to pledge your assets as collateral for the loan."

"Why in the hell do I have to go through all of that crap?" Dick Dick said. "Just give me the loan for two or three days and I'll give it back to you with interest. Sweet and simple and nobody needs to be any the wiser."

"If it was up to me, that's the way we'd do it," Sleepy said, "but it's not up to me. The Federal Reserve and the Banking Commission have these silly rules – they want loans to be secured, especially loans for over three million dollars."

"So, what if we don't follow the rules this one time, what the hell would that hurt?" Dick Dick snarled.

"It's the bank auditors," Sleepy explained. "They check everything - all of our loans and investments and everything else to see if we're in compliance. They'd find it for sure and then the bank would be subject to fines and penalties and probably nasty articles in the newspapers. We can't do it, Dick Dick. You need to pledge your assets as security for the loan."

"So, you're going to tie up every damn thing that I own?" Dick Dick said.

"It's not me, Dick Dick," Sleepy said. "It's nothing personal, it's just the banking rules."

"Well, I don't like following rules," Dick Dick said.

Lenny jumped into the foray. "Dick Dick, it's just like when your clients buy a house, they need collateral in order to get their loan. The same thing applies here to you. But, it will only be for a few days, so why get your pants in a bunch."

"Okay, you guys win," Dick Dick said. "Tomorrow morning I'll bring in the deeds, the titles, and everything else you'll need. Just get the money ready," Dick Dick said.

"I've already got the money ready for you, and I can transfer it to the Land Trust with the push of a button," Sleepy said.

"Well, then, we're all set," Dick Dick said with a broad smile. "Tomorrow could be the most important day of our lives."

Chapter
15

Gat stood between the Dry Dock and Waters Edge Condominiums and admired the serenity of the scene before him. The Dry Dock deck was full of people leisurely enjoying a cocktail and the company of one another as the sound of laughter filled the air. Several boaters were tying up at the dock and another boatload was just heading back out onto the lake.

The sun was reddish orange and in another fifteen minutes it would melt into the horizon. But now it was at the perfect angle to cast a long red glow across the shimmering blue waters of West Lake Okoboji. The sign in front of the Four Seasons Resort said *Fantastic Sunsets!* but those two words didn't come close to describing the brilliance that Gat witnessed before him. It was a scene that could inspire poets to find just the right words to describe the mysteries of life or that could take men who didn't know the difference between love and lust and turn them into hopeless romantics.

Gat walked toward the steps leading down to the dock

so he could watch the sun's final descent from the end of the dock.

"Hey, Rhode Island," someone yelled from behind Gat.

He turned around, searching for the person that the voice belonged to.

"Up here."

Four people were waving to him from the second story deck of the condo. It was Patrick Swayze's look-a-like and his group. "Come on up," they yelled.

Gat climbed the spiral staircase and by the time he reached the deck a cold drink was waiting for him.

They re-introduced themselves, "Bev, Dave, Barb and Bob, also known as Patrick Swayze – and Gat."

The conversation was light-hearted and every five or ten minutes another of the condo neighbors stopped by to say hello, to help themselves to a cold drink, or to deliver a concoction they had whipped up and wanted everyone to sample. And, of course, nearly everyone had a riddle for them to try to solve.

Jeff and Melissa offered this gem: "A man checked out of his hotel room and turned in his key. When housekeeping went to clean his room, they found it locked and dead bolted from the inside. When the manager used his passkey, he found the security chain latched from the inside. All the windows were locked from the inside. How did the man get out of the room?"

And then Jeff and Melissa said, "Think about it, we'll be

back," and they were gone.

The next-door neighbors, the McMahons, overheard the riddle and said, "We own a motel and we know exactly how he did it, but we don't want to spoil your fun, so we won't tell you." No amount of begging would change their minds.

The five of them, Gat and his four hosts, were actually able to solve some of the riddles offered to them. The next-door neighbors, the Throwers, asked, "What is the most frequently used letter of the alphabet?" *Letter "e."*

The Hansons asked, "Andy was born on June 7, 2009. Exactly how old will he be on June 7, 2010?" *One Year and One Day.*

The Tiefenthalers said, "Name two people who did not have belly buttons." *Adam and Eve.*

The party spilled over onto the lawn in front of the condo and some of the downstairs condo neighbors, the O'Donoghues, McHughs, and Klohs felt obligated to welcome this Easterner to Okoboji, which they did by insisting that he join them for a drink or some food.

"Well, how did the guy get out of the hotel room?" Jeff asked as he and Melissa joined the party on the lawn.

"His friend occupied the adjoining room and there were doors between the rooms," Gat said. "He exited through his friend's adjoining room."

"That's damn good work, Gatlin," Jeff said. "You want to join our Great Okoboji Treasure Hunt team?"

"Sorry," Gat said, "but I don't know enough about the area to be of any help to you, but thanks for asking."

Gat sought out Bob, Barb, Dave, and Bev to thank them for the good time. "The other three of you are probably going to be mad at me for saying this," he said to Barb, Bev, and Dave, "but Bob, on second thought, I think you look a lot more like B.J. Thomas than Patrick Swayze."

The four of them broke out laughing. "Thank you," Barb said. "Ever since we tried to convince Bob that he looks like Patrick Swayze, he hasn't been himself, so we'll be glad to have good ol' B.J. Thomas back amongst us."

Bob smiled and said, "I feel like Raindrops Are Falling On My Head."

❖ ❖ ❖

It was shortly after midnight when Gat returned to his room at the Four Seasons Motel. It had been a whirlwind day that started early when Dick Dick had rolled him out of bed to invite him to breakfast and was ending now some eighteen hours later. It had been a full day, and it had been a good day. He had met numerous kind, wonderful, interesting, and colorful people, including the unforgettable blonde and redhead. Even though he was a stranger just passing through town, everyone treated him as though they had known him forever.

The folks at the Iowa Welcome Center had said, "Okoboji is a magical place." The sign at the Chamber of Commerce Office said, "A Great Place To Live, Work, and Play." You expect comments like that from a community's welcome center and from its Chamber of Commerce, but Gat believed that they actually meant it and that they believed it to be true. And, after being in Okoboji for only two days, he was also beginning to believe it. *A Magical Place. A Great Place To Live, Work, and Play.* That pretty well summed it up.

Gat checked that the patio door was locked and that the curtains were drawn tight. He sat down on the edge of his bed, pulled out his cell phone, and dialed a number. A moment later he uttered a cryptic message, "Progress has been made."

Gat quickly deleted the number that he had dialed. He got into bed and turned out the light on the nightstand. He fell asleep wondering what Okoboji might have in store for him tomorrow.

Chapter
16

Dick Dick was an early riser by nature but on this particular day of destiny he was up earlier than usual, at 4 a.m. He showered and carefully selected the perfect outfit to wear that struck the proper balance between being appropriate for boating but that still projected a businesslike image of prosperity and power.

Dick Dick created an acronym to help him remember the major points of his sales presentation in the proper order, LACLUA. L = Location. A = Availability. C = Cost. L = Labor. U = Utilities. A = Amenities.

He rehearsed his presentation in front of the mirror more than a dozen times until he was convinced that it was flawless in both content and delivery. He was good. Damn good.

Dick Dick checked the clock, only 6:10. He grabbed the phone and then put it down. Moments later he grabbed the phone again and put it down again. He was eager to get it started but he knew that he needed to rein in his emotions, to get control of himself, and to let reason and judgment be his guide. His motive for inviting Gatlin for a boat ride was for business purposes only, but he needed to make it appear to Gatlin, at least at the outset, that it was just another friendly social invitation.

Finally, at 7:15 Dick Dick could no longer restrain himself and he dialed the Four Seasons Resort.

Gat was awake but hadn't gotten out of bed yet when the phone rang. He let it ring four times before he answered, "Hello."

"It's a fabulous Okoboji morning, Gatlin Guthrie of Rhode Island," the voice said.

"Dick Dick, is that you?" Gat asked.

"Sorry to call so late in the morning," he said. "I know you like to get up earlier, like you did yesterday."

"I got up very early yesterday," Gat agreed.

"Gatlin, how would you like to go for a boat ride around the fabulous Iowa Great Lakes?"

"At 7:15 in the morning?" Gat asked.

"No, I just wanted to catch you before you left your room this morning. I've got a few details to take care of and then the new clue for this week's treasure hunt is at ten, so how about going boating at, say, noon," Dick Dick said.

"Noon would be great," Gat said. "I really appreciate your offer. Will the other Wise Men be coming along?"

"I don't think so," Dick Dick said. "We've almost got this week's treasure hunt figured out and if we get just a little bit more information, we think we can crack it. So, as soon as the clue is announced, we'll put our heads together and if we can solve it, we'll have that treasure claimed by eleven. But, if we can't crack it, then Sleepy and Lenny will be out digging holes in the ground all afternoon looking for it."

"Where should I meet you?" Gat asked.

"Be at the end of the Dry Dock's dock at noon," Dick Dick said. "I'll pick you up by boat."

❖ ❖ ❖

At precisely 8:30, Dick Dick phoned Punky Cox. Punky was a notorious late riser, at least by Dick Dick's standards, and he prided himself on not having set an alarm for the past dozen years. Every day was a Saturday and he got up when he got up – it was as simple as that.

Punky answered the phone on the third ring.

"Punky, this is Dick Dick. I have wonderful news. I have a client who might be interested in buying that land of yours, all 960 acres."

He let it sink in for a moment before he continued. He would not even ask Punky if he was interested in selling. He would use the *Assumption Close,* assuming that Punky wanted to sell the land, assuming that Punky would sell it through Dick Dick Realty, assuming that Punky would sell it at a reasonable price, assuming that Punky would be able to make a decision on Dick Dick's timetable, assuming that Punky would pay the full sales commission, always assuming, assuming, assuming.

"Who?" Punky asked.

The question was music to Dick Dick's trained ears. He was interested. "The buyer is a land trust and the names of the individuals are not revealed in a land trust."

"They'll have to pay full price, not a penny less," Punky said firmly.

"Let's see," Dick Dick said, "you wanted what – five million for the 960 acres."

"Dick Dick, like I've always told you, that's one of the most unique pieces of land in this whole part of the state for an industrial site. The price is ten million."

Punky's firmness and forcefulness surprised Dick Dick. Normally, Punky preferred to launch into a lengthy dissertation of the underlying forces that affected and influenced his thinking and reasoning that led to his ultimate conclusion. But today, not so. Boom – Punky wanted his ten million, period.

"I'll see what I can do," Dick Dick said.

"Where's the buyer from?" Punky asked.

"Punky, until you sign a listing agreement agreeing to pay my commission if I sell the land, I'm not going to tell you anything more."

Dick Dick had been through this a hundred times before with potential sellers that he approached about selling their property who wanted to weasel out of him the name of the buyer so they could bypass him and not pay the sales commission.

"Speaking of the sales commission, Dick Dick, I'm not

paying one," Punky said. "Either get the buyer to pay you a finder's fee or tack on a couple hundred thousand to the sales price for yourself, but I want ten million net. For Molly and me."

"Everybody pays a sales commission, Punky. You know that."

"Nope, not this time. Not by me. Not by Molly and me," Punky said. "Like I told you, get the buyer to pay a finder's fee."

Dick Dick wished that Punky wouldn't keep bringing up Molly's name. That had been a long time ago and it had ended poorly. He would just as soon never think about it, or her, again.

"I don't think that'll fly," Dick Dick said, "but I'll run it up the flagpole and see."

"I'm going to listen to the Treasure Hunt clue at 10:00, and then I'm going to go out and claim the treasure," Punky said with the type of bravado that had become common banter and good natured teasing among the various treasure hunters. "Call me on my cell phone if you get an offer on the land – and remember, ten million, net."

Dick Dick had known Punky Cox for many years and had always considered him to be an intellectual snob who could talk a good game but who could never cut it in the real world. He was too soft. Too theoretical. He could never stand toe to toe with an adversary and slug it out until the best man won. That, in fact, Punky was not a real man at all. A wimp. But here, today, Punky had stood firm. And with every sense in his trained salesman's body, he knew that Punky Cox meant it. It was ten million net, or nothing. Dick Dick made a mental note to never again call Punky before ten in the morning, he was just too damned ornery when you woke him up and rolled him out of bed.

❖ ❖ ❖

Dick Dick arrived at Sleepy's bank shortly before nine o'clock. "That Punky's a real prick," he said.

"When he's been out drinking wine he's ornery as hell the next morning until he has a Bloody Mary – that mellows him out," Sleepy said.

"I tried to get him to take five million for the land, but he wants ten million, net – and he won't pay a real estate commission. Like I said, he's a real prick," Dick Dick said. "And you and Lenny knew I was going to split the commission with the two of you – right?"

"Ya, right," Sleepy said sarcastically. "Well, we were planning on paying around ten million for Punky's land, so we're right on target. By the way, did you get hold of Gatlin?"

"It's all set – I pick him up at noon for the boat ride," Dick Dick said. "This is going to be a day we'll remember the rest of our lives."

"This will put us on the map," Sleepy said with a dry smile.

Dick Dick opened his briefcase and removed a stack of

deeds, titles, stock certificates, and mutual fund statements. "There it is – everything I own, totaling about three and a half million dollars."

"Including the title to your Bentley convertible?" Sleepy asked.

"Even title to the Bentley," Dick Dick said. "Of all the things that I own, the Bentley is my pride and joy. You can see how convinced I am that this is going to work."

"I believe it will," Sleepy said. "And if Gatlin doesn't want to build his CIA building here in Okoboji or if he won't buy Punky's land for the twenty million we need, well, we'll still be where we are right now – no harm done. Right?"

"That's right," Dick Dick said. "It's foolproof. There are lots of ways we can win, but there's no way we can lose."

Dick Dick signed the assignment forms that Lenny had prepared and handed over ownership to his entire financial empire.

"Lenny's coming here for the reading of the clue at ten, right?" Dick Dick asked.

"He said he'll be here," Sleepy replied.

"I have a feeling that not only will this deal with Gatlin go together but that we're going to solve the Treasure Hunt riddle today also. A day to remember," Dick Dick said.

❖ ❖ ❖

The Arnolds Park Public Library is located in the city's all-purpose municipal building that also houses the police department, Mayor's office, city offices, and fire trucks.

They parked the Cadillac convertible two blocks away so if anyone in city hall had seen the blonde and the redhead in the car last night they would not be inclined to make the obvious connection.

No one would have been able to make the connection between the blonde and the redhead and these two by their appearance this morning, though. Where the blonde and the redhead were sexy, erotic, sassy, and flashy – bordering on trashy, these two resembled meek and mild choir girls or maybe a couple of sheltered small town elementary school teachers on a once-a-month outing to have a big time downing a couple glasses of iced tea.

The former blonde, Michelle, wore a loose fitting pale yellow dress that came two inches below her knees. Her long black hair was tied back and she wore reading glasses with thin black plastic frames that she had purchased just this morning at Wal-Mart. She looked professional, competent, businesslike, and believable. She could easily have passed for a television news anchor, which was the image she was trying to portray.

The former redhead, Courtney, wore a light blue silk blouse, tan dress slacks, and brown leather shoes with low heels. Her short auburn hair was combed back and she, like Michelle, wore only a limited amount of carefully applied makeup. She looked like someone who would fit right in, standing in the middle of a field talking about exotic weeds. At least, that's the way the two of them saw it.

They approached the counter and Michele asked quietly, "Are you the librarian, Sue?"

"Yes, I am," she said.

"Could you tell us where we can find Mr. Watts?" Courtney asked.

"Yes, he's back in that corner," Sue said, motioning to the back of the library.

A man was sitting at a table with a half dozen open books spread out before him. He wore a short-sleeved plaid shirt, jeans, and white tennis shoes. His black hair was disheveled and he wore black plastic glasses similar to Michelle's except his rims were about four times as wide as hers. This geek, this nerd, obviously was not the movie producer from New York City. But he was probably the producer's assistant and would know where they could find him.

They watched the man pour over the books for a moment until he sensed their presence. "May I help you?"

"Can you tell us where we can find Mr. Watts?" Courtney asked.

"Why do you want to see him?" he asked. It was apparent that the producer's time was valuable and that not everyone would be considered worthy to stand in his presence. It was also apparent that this assistant's job was to screen out the unworthy.

"We understand that Mr. Watts is going to produce a documentary for National Public Television and that he will be using two people from the area to appear in his film," Michelle said.

"We would like to talk to him about his project and audition for it," Courtney added.

"I see," the geek said. "Do either of you have acting experience?"

"No, we don't, but we can learn," Michelle said.

"Turn sideways," the geek ordered.

They obeyed.

"Now make a quarter turn so your backs are to me."

Again, they obeyed.

"And now another quarter turn so I can see your left profile – and now turn and face me."

They turned to face him and found him watching them through a rectangle that he had formed by touching the thumbs and middle fingers of his hands together. Obviously the geek was trying to make them think he was simulating the lens of a movie camera. It appeared that they had no choice but to play along with this weirdo if they wanted to get past him and audition for Mr. Watts.

The geek handed Michelle a sheet of paper with words on it and asked her to read.

"Before the settlers cleared the land for farming, and before the plow, there were thousands and thousands of square miles of prairie grass, and exotic prairie plants. But that was more than two hundred years ago and now . . . ."

"That's enough," he said to Michelle.

And she thought she was doing so good. She just hoped that Mr. Watts wasn't as rude as this geek and that he would grant her an appropriate audition to let her show what she could do. But she had read some movie magazines and she had heard some stories about the movie industry and she was aware that it could be ruthless. Well, if this geek thought he was going to get her on the casting couch, well, she'd let him have it, alright, a knuckle sandwich right in the middle of those black rimmed glasses.

Courtney was next to read, "The settlers can't be blamed for tilling the prairie. They had crops to plant, families and animals to feed, and lives to live. But now, virgin prairie, never touched by the plow, is one of America's most endangered species. In fact there may be as little as one thousand . . . ."

"That's fine. That's enough," the geek said.

He stared at them for a moment, apparently trying to decide if they were worthy of being passed on to the next stage of the audition process, with the producer himself.

"Filming will begin a week from Monday," he said. "It's a rigorous schedule, starting at 6 a.m. and going until sunset. We expect to wrap the project in five days of filming. Pay is $2,500 a day for each of you plus residuals of $500 each for every time the program is aired on any television station. There will be a private room at Fillenwarth Beach for each of you during the week of filming and a per diem of $75 each for food. A contract will be drawn specifying these terms that you will need to sign the morning we begin shooting. Any questions?"

"Yes," Michelle said. "Don't we have to talk to Mr. Watts before we pass the audition?"

He looked from one of them to the other and smiled.

173

"Michelle, Courtney, I'm Charles Watts. I'm the producer and the director, and you're hired. See you a week from Monday, 6 a.m. sharp right here in the city hall parking lot."

All of a sudden, they saw this guy in a different light. He wasn't a geek or a weirdo after all; he was an artist, a creative genius. And he was better looking than he first appeared, much better. And there was a certain flair and sophistication about him. They had been fooled by the handsome, smooth, debonair Gatlin Guthrie who turned out not to be a movie producer. But now they were standing there staring at the real thing, a real live movie producer. Staring. They were too stunned and embarrassed to say anything other than to mutter, "See you a week from Monday morning. And, thank you, Mr. Watts."

Michelle and Courtney turned and quietly began to walk away.

"One more thing," he said.

"Yes," "Yes," they both said eagerly, waiting for further instructions from The Producer.

"That was a very impressive performance at the Barefoot Bar last night," he said as a matter of fact, and then he returned his attention to the sprawl of books in front of him.

They stood for a moment, looking at each other, not knowing if they should respond or not and finally, not being able to think of anything appropriate to say, they tiptoed out the door.

They walked a block before either of them said a word.

"He's a real professional."

"He observes everything that goes on around him. He doesn't miss a single thing."

"Apparently."

"We should feel honored to be working with such greatness."

"As movie stars."

"As exotic movie stars."

"Exotic native prairie plant movie stars!"

"It's got a nice ring to it."

Chapter

17

It was five minutes to ten and every radio in Okoboji was tuned to KUOO for Clue Number Three. The first two clues had been easier to decipher than for most of the weekly Treasure Hunts, so there were high hopes of solving the riddle by about 10:05 and of claiming the treasure, and the bragging rights, by about 10:20. It had been widely discussed over a brew or two - which was the most important thing in the Treasure Hunt – claiming the $1,000 prize or claiming the bragging rights? Most seemed to agree that the $1,000 might not last beyond the weekend, but that the bragging rights would last a lifetime, and maybe even be carried on from generation to generation.

"Good morning, Okoboji. This is KUOO radio; I'm Chad Taylor. It's ten o'clock Saturday morning and you know what that means – it's time for Clue Number Three in this week's Great Okoboji Treasure Hunt. Two heavily armed uniformed police officers are standing by with today's clue. But first, here's a warm-up for you – and whoever calls in first with the correct answer will receive a free dinner for two from Captain's Getaway in Arnolds Park. Just call 712-336-KUOO – that's 712-336-5866. Now, here's today's warm-up – 'If you walk on me when I'm living I won't make a sound, but if you walk on me when I'm dead, believe me, you'll hear from me. What am I?' If you think you know the answer, call 336-5866."

"I know the answer, I know the answer," Sleepy yelled as he grabbed the phone and dialed. He got the busy signal. He continued to hit the redial button as he listened to the idiotic answers being called in.

"Bones," "A paper bag," "Plastic," "Matchsticks," "Straw . . ."

"Leaves," Sleepy yelled, as much to impress Lenny and Dick Dick as anything. "The answer is *leaves*." He continued to hit redial but the line was still busy.

Finally, he heard the word that he dreaded. "Leaves," a caller said. And, predictably, the announcer heaped praise upon the caller, praise that should have been Sleepy's.

"And now, before I read Clue Number Three to this week's Great Okoboji Treasure Hunt, I will review Clues Number One and Two. Clue Number One was: 'Sometimes our best plans fall, because we think too small. And that could be true of me – me in all my majesty.' Clue Number Two was: 'You've seen me a time or three, but probably paid me very little heed. Every day you depend on me; I've got what you want and what you need.'

"And now for Clue Number Three: 'Day or night, here's

what I do, I stand watch over you. But there's more to me than that; take all you want, you won't get fat.'"

He repeated the clue twice more, slowly, so everyone could write it down.

"And there you have it, Clue Number Three. Good luck, and now we return to our regular programming with an appropriate song for today, "She's A Mystery," by the band, Time Wounds All Heels."

The Three Wise Men had recorded the clue and they were now listening to the replay for the third time.

"I've got it!" Sleepy shouted. "It's a water tower – the treasure certificate is hidden at a water tower."

"I think it might be a billboard or a tank at the Fish Hatchery in Spirit Lake," Dick Dick said.

"That makes no sense at all," Sleepy said. "Look at the clues. *You think too small – me in all my majesty.'* What's bigger and more majestic than a water tower?

"And another clue – *You've seen me but paid me no heed.'* We drive by a water tower ten times a day and don't even notice it.

"And another clue says, *'Every day you depend on me – I've got what you need.'* Well, we depend on water every day and we need it.

"But the clinchers are from today's clue – *'I stand watch over you.'* That's a water tower. And *'Take all you want, you won't get fat.'* What else besides water can you take all you want and not get fat?

"It's got to be a water tower," Sleepy said. "Let's go claim our treasure."

"I still think it might be at the Fish Hatchery," Dick Dick said.

"Look, I solved the warm-up puzzle about the leaves and I've got a feeling that I'm right about this one, too. I'm on my game today. It's a water tower. It has to be."

"I think Sleepy might be right," Lenny said. "But, there are a dozen water towers in the Okoboji area, which one?"

Not wanting to be cast as the naysayer that cost The Three Wise Men the solution to the Treasure Hunt, Dick Dick jumped on the bandwagon. "If it's a water tower, it would have to be the one in Arnolds Park by the city park," he said. "The Chamber would want it to be somewhere visible where a lot of people might witness the finder locating the treasure, so they can make a big deal out of it, not somewhere remote where no will see it."

"What have we got to lose?" Lenny said, "Let's go check it out."

They were half a block from the Arnolds Park water tower when they saw it – two people jumping out of a pick-up truck that was still rolling and another car coming to a screeching, sliding halt next to the pickup. By the time The Three Wise Men got out of Dick Dick's Escalade, some goofy guy was already yelling and screaming that he had found the treasure.

That was twice within fifteen minutes that Sleepy had demonstrated the same genius that had created the South-worth fortune and that had made the Southworth name legendary in the state of South Dakota. And he had been within seconds each time of claiming the prize and of receiving the praise and admiration that he truly deserved. Yes, today he was on top of his game, and it was a good omen.

He had a feeling that everything was going to go his way today and that the Defense Department CIA building was going to be a lead pipe cinch. How could they lose? If Gatlin Guthrie didn't want to play ball, it would cost them nothing; they would end up exactly where they started, and they would have had a little fun along the way. But, if Dick Dick were able to work his sales magic on Gatlin Guthrie, they would make millions and millions and millions and be widely loved and admired. He was on top of his game today. It was a good omen.

Chapter

18

Dick Dick admired the flawless condition of his boat. The detailers had done a good job, especially on such short notice. But, today it would be more than a boat; it would be a floating office where he would consummate the most brilliant transaction of his illustrious real estate career.

By most standards, the crown jewel of the Iowa Great Lakes, West Lake Okoboji, is a small lake, being perhaps four miles wide and seven miles long with a circumference of twenty-six miles. Access to East Lake Okoboji is gained by boating under two bridges that can be quite low when the water level is high. From East Lake Okoboji, boaters can reach Upper Gar, Minnewashta, and Lower Gar lakes by passing under fairly low bridges where the waters of one lake flow to the next.

In a resort area like Okoboji, a boat is one of the three most visible signs of wealth and prestige, right behind one's house and tied with one's automobile. Therefore, on West Lake Okoboji, even though the lake technically might be too small for such large vessels, there are numerous cabin cruisers over thirty-five feet long, costing hundreds of thousands of dollars.

By nature, Dick Dick prides himself on having the biggest, the best, and the most. He takes great pleasure in having things that others cannot afford, or if they can afford them, that they cannot bring themselves to go ahead and buy. Therefore, when it came to boats, it would have been in character for Dick Dick to quiz every marina operator in Okoboji to determine what was the biggest and most expensive boat they had ever sold, and to then order one bigger and more expensive. But, when it came to buying a boat, Dick Dick acted out of character.

Dick Dick hates cabin cruisers. First of all, although he would never admit it because it might be interpreted as a sign of weakness, he suffers from motion sickness and even the thought of sleeping overnight on a boat makes him queasy. Second, Dick Dick likes to be where the action is and with many cabin cruisers, the captain is on the upper deck steering the boat and the action is down on the lower deck. His final reason is that when the water is high, it is sometimes impossible to get a cabin cruiser of the size he would have bought under the bridges into East Lake Okoboji and passing under the bridges to the other three lakes is out of the question. Since Dick Dick regularly uses his boat to show property to prospects from lakeside, a cabin cruiser would be worthless about half of the time. And besides that, if he were up there steering the boat, he couldn't be down there patting them on the back and becoming their new best friend.

So, Dick Dick's boat isn't as expensive as some of the cabin cruisers out on the lake, but it was the most expensive open bow Cobalt ever sold in the state of Iowa. So, not totally out of character, after all.

Gat was waiting on the Four Seasons' dock when Dick Dick pulled up. He jumped on board and they were off.

Dick Dick had carefully created his game plan starting with a leisurely cruise close to the shoreline while he pointed out magnificent houses owned by prominent families from Sioux Falls, Sioux City, Des Moines, Minneapolis, Cedar Rapids, Kansas City, Topeka, Omaha, Chicago, and places in between. "A surgeon lives there, the president of the world's largest manufacturer of nuts and bolts lives there, a banker lives there, a hotel magnate lives there, a U.S. Senator lives there, a bestselling author lives there, the founder of a chain of gas stations lives there." Every house was occupied by someone who was rich or famous, or both.

Today, it was eighty degrees, the sun was shining, there was a slight breeze, and it would be hard to find a more perfect day anywhere on the planet. Dick Dick made sure not to mention that in the winter the temperature can stay below freezing for a month or more at a time, that the snow can come at you sideways, and that the snow might start piling up in November and not disappear until May.

"Tell me, Gatlin, what do you think of our little paradise here in Okoboji?" Dick Dick asked.

"I love it. I absolutely love it," Gat said. "I haven't been everywhere but I've been a lot of places – Aspen, Martha's Vineyard, The Hamptons, the Gulf Coast - but Okoboji is special. Beryl at the Welcome Center said that Okoboji is a magical place and I really think that is true."

Perfect. Dick Dick couldn't have written a better script himself. It was time to make his move.

"Gatlin, I was curious, so I did a little research and I found out that you have had a lot of success with government contracts," Dick Dick said.

Gat smiled. "Well, I guess I should be flattered that you were curious enough to check me out. It's a matter of public record that I've been fortunate enough to land some sizable government contracts of various kinds."

"Let's talk business," Dick Dick said. "I have a strong suspicion that you have another government contract in the works and that you're on your way to Kansas and Colorado to select a site." He paused for a moment. Gat didn't confirm or deny it.

"I'm listening," Gat said.

"Well, I was thinking," Dick Dick said. "Whatever they can offer in Kansas or Colorado we can offer here in Okoboji, and better." He remembered the acronym for his sales pitch, LACLUA, and he launched into a flawless description of each: Location, Availability, Cost, Labor, Utilities, and Amenities. And every aspect of his sales pitch pointed to one final conclusion, Gatlin should buy the 960 acres from the Okoboji Beneficial Land Trust and build his new government project there.

"That's a very impressive and very persuasive presentation," Gat said, "but you probably wasted your breath."

Dick Dick's heart sunk. He had given Gatlin his best shot. He had asked every question and raised every objection that Gatlin could possibly raise and he had answered each before Gatlin had a chance to bring them up. Had he missed something?

"Why's that?" Dick Dick asked, trying not to show his disappointment and trying not to reveal that he was thinking of throwing this damned Easterner overboard.

"Well, this morning after you called, I went back out to that industrial site that you showed me yesterday and I spent a couple of hours checking it out. I even bought a shovel and dug a few holes to see what the soil looked like – clay and sand just like you said."

Dick Dick's hopes soared. Was he actually hearing what he thought he was hearing? Was it leading where he thought it might lead?

"And?" Dick Dick said.

"And I was thinking all of the same things that you just said," Gat said. "I did some research yesterday at the Chamber of Commerce office and at the library and got a lot of information about utility rates, the labor pool, the local work ethic, the local amenities for the work force, schools - all that sort of thing. The more I learned, the more convinced I became that Okoboji would be a great site for my new project."

Dick Dick almost grabbed Gatlin and hugged him. This was going exactly like he had played it out in his mind. It was now time to tie down the details.

"The 960 acres are available, twenty million," Dick Dick said, following his own rule to never attach the word, "dollars," to the amount when talking to a prospective buyer.

"There would be two contingencies," Gat said. "First, I would need a written commitment from the county that they would deed to me that unimproved road between the two parcels of ground so it becomes all one parcel."

"No problem," Dick Dick said. "I've already proposed that to the County Engineer and the county is eager to do it just to get rid of the headache and the potential liability. And, the second contingency?"

"Zoning," Gat said. "My offer would be contingent upon the county approving the land for use for my project. I will not reveal the exact use of the land until the sales contract is signed by the seller and then I will reveal it in detail before I sign, so the seller can still back out if they want to. However, I will verify right now that it is a federal government project, that it will bring more than five thousand people to the site and that there will be many highly paid jobs provided by this project. It is clean, with no pollution to the air or water and it would be a permanent site for at least fifty years and probably beyond."

Dick Dick smiled to himself. Five thousand jobs! Everything was falling together exactly like he had planned. And the contingency - this was common in every commercial real estate contract that he had ever written.

"No problem," Dick Dick said. "I'll put both of those

contingencies in the contract. And, I'm absolutely positive that neither of them will present any problem."

Everything was sailing along unbelievably smooth, but there was one more potential land mine lying ahead. Dick Dick had experienced it many times. The buyer agrees that "Yes, this is a good deal," "Yes, he should do this," "Yes, he can afford it," "Yes, he wants to do it," "Yes, Yes, Yes," but for some reason he's afraid to pull the trigger.

Dick Dick reached for his briefcase, opened it, and removed a manila file folder. It was time to again use his favorite sales tactic, the Assumption Close. Gatlin had said that he was willing to buy the property, now Dick Dick assumed that he would be willing to sign a short form of the contract, called a *binder*, that would clearly indicate his serious intentions of going ahead with the transaction and would, in fact, bind him to the general terms of the agreement until the formal contract could be drawn.

Dick Dick completed the binder, briefly describing the 960-acre parcel, the twenty million dollar sales price, the two contingencies, and the names of the seller and the buyer.

Gat read the binder carefully. "Everything looks in order," he said, and he whipped out his pen and signed it.

Another of Dick Dick's self-imposed sales rules was, after the buyer signs the contract, don't say "Thank You," but instead, say, "Congratulations." After all, he had just done the buyer a favor and the buyer should actually thank him, if anybody was going to thank anybody. Another of his rules was, after the contract is signed, don't hang around and play footsie with the buyer. Wrap it up and get the hell out of there before the buyer starts asking a bunch of stupid questions or buyer's remorse sets in and they want to back out of the deal.

Within ten minutes Dick Dick deposited Gatlin at the Four Seasons Resort with plans to meet at Dick Dick Realty at eight tonight to sign the formal contract and to take care of the details. Dick Dick said he would have liked to meet at an earlier hour, but that he had an appointment with another client that might take all afternoon.

Gatlin promised to bring his file showing the blueprint of the planned government development. Dick Dick promised to bring the updated abstract showing clear title to the land. Dick Dick would have the formal sales agreement completed for Gatlin and the Okoboji Beneficial Land Trust agent, who happened to be Lenny, to sign.

On Monday morning, the County Board of Supervisors would meet and Dick Dick was certain that they would quickly approve the two contingencies, clearing the way for title to be transferred to Gatlin for his CIA development. Then, later on Monday morning Gatlin and Dick Dick would meet and the twenty million dollars would be transferred to the Okoboji Beneficial Land Trust, the deed would be given to Gatlin and it would be over. And, Dick Dick's net worth would double.

Dick Dick decided not to try any fancy footwork with Punky to try to pry a sales commission out of him or to try to get him to lower his sales price. He had tried that with a deal a couple of years ago and it all fell apart and he lost what would have been a surefire eighty thousand dollar commission. He was not about to repeat that performance and lose a surefire three million. A surefire three point three three three million.

Punky answered his cell phone on the second ring. Dick Dick liked that; it showed he was eager.

"I have good news, Punky my friend," he said. "I have an offer in hand for the full ten million dollars!" With a buyer, he never used the word, "dollars," but with the seller he always did. It gave a lot more punch to the amount.

"Maybe I asked too little," Punky said.

"What an ungrateful prick," Dick Dick said to himself. But, he had heard this comment a hundred times, often from sellers who had their property on the market for over a year and who finally got an offer. There was some strange psychology at play here that Dick Dick wasn't even going to try to understand.

"Got you the full price, can't do any better than that," Dick Dick said, ignoring Punky's idiotic comment.

"When do I get the money?" Punky asked.

Another good sign. "I have a signed contract in my office and I will have a cashier's check for you."

"No," Punky said, and Dick Dick's heart almost stopped for the second time today.

"I want an electronic funds transfer. Half to Molly's account in Gulf Shores, Alabama, and half to my account. And I want them today."

"That should be no problem," Dick Dick said, relieved to have dodged another bullet. "I'll have Sleepy take care of it. Let's meet at Sleepy's bank in, say, an hour."

"I'll be there," Punky said.

Dick Dick made a quick phone call to Lenny and Sleepy who were anxiously waiting at Sleepy's bank. "It's all set. Gatlin went for the deal – twenty million dollars! Lenny, get the deed ready. Sleepy, put the ten million in the Land Trust account and get ready to make two five million dollar wire transfers. Punky will be there in an hour. I'll be there in a half hour."

❖ ❖ ❖

They were giddy. The plan was working to perfection. Only a few minor details, like paying out ten million dollars and collecting twenty million dollars remained. By noon Monday, it would be done.

Punky arrived right on time. Even though Dick Dick more or less despised Punky, Lenny looked down on him, and Sleepy tolerated him, they treated him cordially and congenially like a long-lost friend. And, although Punky had come to realize that the three of them were not true friends, he reciprocated by being gracious and friendly. Each side secretly knew that they were getting the best of the other side and they were all afraid to breathe for fear they might foul up the deal at the last minute.

The closing of the deal took only a few minutes. Lenny

produced deeds to the two parcels of land, which were signed by LeRoy Cox, Punky's real name, and also signed by LeRoy Cox as power of attorney for Molly Cox.

Punky gave Sleepy his and Molly's bank account routing numbers, Sleepy pushed a few keys on his computer, and announced that five million dollars had been routed to each account.

Punky called his sister on his cell phone and told her to log on and check her bank account balance – the five million was there. Punky borrowed one of the bank's computers and checked his own account balance – it had five million dollars more than it had this morning. Punky handed over the deed, shook hands with the three of them, promised to see them at the Thursday afternoon card game at The Gardens and left.

Chapter
19

When Gatlin Guthrie hadn't arrived at Dick Dick Realty by 8:05, The Three Wise Men started to get nervous. When he hadn't shown by 8:10, they started pacing the floor, and when it hit 8:15, they were ready to swear out a missing person's report with the Sheriff. When he walked in the door at 8:16 carrying his briefcase, they almost kissed his feet.

He had taken a wrong turn, Gat said, and being a stranger here, took another wrong turn trying to get back on track, and with lakes everywhere, there are very few roads that run straight to anywhere. It was a common problem for strangers in Okoboji and The Three Wise Men said that they understood fully.

Dick Dick was dressed in a splendid light grey suit with dark grey stripes, complimented by a red necktie with light grey stripes. Look prosperous, you know. Lenny wore a knit golf shirt and casual tan slacks and looked every bit the slick and successful attorney that he was. Sleepy was dressed in name brand clothes that can't be bought within two hundred miles of Okoboji, but he looked like the clothes had been thrown on him with a shovel. Gatlin was dressed in a flowered short sleeve shirt and light grey slacks and looked every bit like a guy who could put together deals for hundreds of millions of dollars.

After a few pleasantries, Dick Dick took control of the meeting and got down to business. He explained to Gatlin that Mr. Rosenthal, Lenny, was there as the agent of the seller, the Okoboji Beneficial Land Trust, and that he had authority to act on the Land Trust's behalf. Mr. Southworth, who Gatlin would recall was a banker, was there in case there were any questions about financial matters.

Mr. Southworth? It was the first time that Dick Dick had ever called him that and Sleepy liked it, although he doubted that this show of respect would extend beyond this night. It was a pleasure watching Dick Dick work. He was pulling out all the stops.

Dick Dick produced a copy of the agreement, which was a legal size sheet of paper with printing on both sides. He said he realized that Gatlin had seen many of these before, but since it was the first Iowa sales agreement that he had ever seen, he felt obligated to read through each item and to explain anything that wasn't clear. That took about fifteen minutes and Gat had no questions.

Dick Dick presented two copies of the sales contract to Lenny, which he signed on behalf of the Okoboji Beneficial Land Trust. Next, Dick Dick presented the two copies of the contract to Gatlin for signing.

"As I mentioned this afternoon on the boat," Gat said, "before I sign the sales agreement, I will reveal to the seller's agent, Mr. Rosenthal, and to you as his sales agent, Dick Dick, the exact nature of the project that I plan to build on this site. Then, after this disclosure, if either of you have any questions or comments, I will be happy to address them. And, if for some reason the seller would prefer not to sell the land for the purpose that I intend, the seller may withdraw their offer to sell the land if they wish and I will be on my way to Kansas and Colorado."

Each of The Three Wise Men had to smile to themselves. Gatlin was being very thorough and generous, even, offering them the chance to back out of the deal after he revealed all of the details of his project. He didn't know it, but they already knew all of the details! No way were they about to walk away from this sweet deal.

Gatlin laid his briefcase on the table – the same briefcase that Lenny had the pleasure of inspecting yesterday morning. This was going to be the good part. The part where Gatlin told them about the Defense Department CIA building and all the other good stuff.

Gat flicked the two latches of the briefcase three times with his thumbs and then, to everyone's amazement, he grabbed each latch and twisted it so that it went from being horizontal to now being vertical. He flicked each latch with his thumbs and a secret compartment opened at the top of the briefcase.

"This is a CIA briefcase," Gat explained. "The Director

of the CIA gave it to me himself."

Reference to the CIA seemed to mesmerize Dick Dick and Sleepy. This is what they had been waiting for. It had a completely different affect on Lenny, however. He was afraid that he was about to see something that he had not seen when he had so carefully inspected the contents of Gatlin's briefcase in his motel room.

Gat reached into the secret compartment and removed an envelope. He withdrew the contents from the envelope and sifted through the half dozen sheets until he found the one he was looking for. It was the blueprint of his new project that was to be built in Okoboji. He spread it out on the table in front of himself and spun it around so that the three of them on the other side of the table could see it.

The words at the top of the blueprint knocked the wind out of Dick Dick and rendered him speechless for one of the few times in his life. The blood drained out of Lenny's face and Sleepy suddenly had the urge to vomit.

UNITED STATES GOVERNMENT – CORREC-TIONS DEPARTMENT – FACILITY FOR THE CRIMI-NALLY INSANE.

Finally, Dick Dick was able eke out a few words, "Wha, Wha, What's this?"

"It's the new facility that I'm planning on building here in Okoboji," Gat replied.

"I, I, I thought you were going to build a Defense Department building," Lenny gasped.

"Li, li, like maybe something for the CIA," Sleepy mumbled, damn near making a confession.

"Where did you get the idea that I was going to build a Defense Department building here – or something for the CIA?" Gat asked with a truly puzzled look on his face.

"You must have said something about it to one of us," Dick Dick said.

"Ya, I think that's right," Sleepy agreed.

"Gentlemen, you know very well that I did not reveal anything at all about my plans, even when you tried very hard to get me to reveal them," Gat said firmly.

The three of them could not refute it.

Gat grabbed an envelope from the bottom of his briefcase, removed a blueprint from it, and laid it on the table in front of them. The heading said, *CONFIDENTIAL – PROPERTY OF THE UNITED STATES GOVERNMENT. INTELLIGENCE DIVISION.*

"Maybe this is what you were thinking of," Gat said. "My company built this facility for the CIA two years ago at a location that I'm not allowed to reveal for security reasons. There was quite a bit of publicity about this project in the media and on the Internet. When you did a background check on me, you probably stumbled across this – that's probably where you got the idea I was going to build a CIA building here in Okoboji."

"Maybe," Dick Dick said somberly.

"I'm not supposed to show this blueprint to anyone, for security reasons," Gat said as he folded it and put it back in the envelope. "But, I thought that you deserved to know since somehow you got the mistaken idea that this was the new project that I was going to build."

The three of them looked down, bewildered and defeated. This couldn't be happening. Not to them. They were The Three Wise Men.

"The facility will house four thousand criminally insane federal prisoners and will employ four hundred psychiatrists and psychologists, along with another six hundred guards and other personnel." Gat said.

"The nature of this project, a correctional facility for the criminally insane, can be pretty controversial. This is why I wanted to make a full and complete disclosure of the nature of the project before I signed the sales agreement and bound the seller to the project," Gat explained.

"We've already been turned down by two communities that thought having such a facility, although it would provide great economic benefits, would place a negative stigma on their community forever.

"Well, does anyone have any questions about this project?" Gat asked.

No one answered.

Gat packed up his materials and closed his briefcase. "This is something, Dick Dick, that you and the owners of the Land Trust will need to study very carefully before deciding what to do. Personally, I would love to build the correctional facility here in Okoboji, but if you decide not to go ahead, I will understand. I'm due to meet with some people in Kansas on Wednesday, so if you want to go ahead here in Okoboji, let me know before then. It was a pleasure meeting all of you. Best of luck."

The Three Wise Men waited until Gat had exited the building and then their pent-up emotions exploded.

"We'll be the scourges of Okoboji. They'll hate us. They'll run us out of town," Sleepy said.

"Hell, they'll run us out of the state," Lenny said.

"We were going to be heroes, people were going to admire us and love us; now we're going to be goats," Sleepy lamented.

"Our careers will be ruined," Lenny said.

"We can't bring all those weirdoes and nuts and crackpots to Okoboji; it would ruin the area," Sleepy said.

"Four thousand criminally insane," Lenny said.

"I was talking about the psychologists and psychiatrists," Sleepy said. "And the prisoners would be almost as bad."

"We can't do it. We just can't do it," Lenny said resolutely. "The repercussions would be devastating."

"That's right," Sleepy agreed. "Let's sell the land to some farmer, take our losses, forget it, and move on."

"Dick Dick, How much can we sell it for?" Lenny asked.

Dick Dick was in a trance. His eyes were wide open in a blank stare, his mouth hung open like a flytrap and his arms hung limply at his sides. He uttered a guttural sound, "Uhl curlm."

"What did you say?" Lenny asked.

"Ull cul em," Dick Dick repeated.

201

Lenny slapped Dick Dick's cheek hard with the palm of his hand and then he backhanded the other cheek. "Snap out of it!" he yelled.

Dick Dick sprang back to life and shouted, "I said I'll kill 'em."

"Who?" Sleepy asked.

"Whoever did this to us. I'll kill 'em," Dick Dick repeated.

"I hate to say this, but we did it to ourselves," Lenny said.

"Let's forget the whole thing before we really get ourselves in trouble and get run out of town," Lenny continued. "Let's sell the land, get what we can out of it, take our hit, and keep our mouths shut about the whole damn mess. We can survive it."

"I agree," Sleepy said. "Let's just forget the whole thing."

"No!" Dick Dick screamed. "There's more to life than surviving. There's got to be a way out of this. I've got to think. I've got to think. I'm going to my boat. I've got to think."

Dick Dick charged out of the office like a mad bull and left Lenny and Sleepy there to lock up the place.

"We cannot do this to Okoboji," Sleepy said.

"We will not do this to Okoboji," Lenny stated firmly.

❖ ❖ ❖

They stood in the dark next to the runway as the twin

engine Cessna taxied toward them.

"I really like Okoboji," Gat said. "If circumstances were a little different, I wouldn't mind spending some time here in the summers, but after tonight . . . ."

"Thanks for your help," his companion said.

"Paybacks can be hell, but I really didn't do anything," Gat said. "I just hung around town and The Three Wise Men did all the work."

"We're even now," his companion said.

"Well, you saved me big time when you took the rap for both of us," Gat said. "Today, it doesn't mean much, but back then it would have created a scandal that might have rocked my whole family's political careers. And it might have kept me from being able to even apply for a government contract. I never forgot it, so I was glad to help out when you called."

"Do you still smoke the weed?" the companion asked.

"Never again, not even once after that night," Gat answered.

"Me neither." They both shared a laugh.

"My plane is waiting. Keep in touch," Gat said as he headed for the Cessna.

"Thanks, again. Travel safe."

❖ ❖ ❖

Dick Dick steered his boat toward open water at a high rate of speed. The night air felt good on his face and it helped him clear his mind to think, to think, to think.

The silence of the evening was broken only by the sound of an airplane overhead as the plane climbed higher and higher until the sound faded away as the plane disappeared from sight, heading southwest.

When the boat reached an open area in the middle of the lake, with no other boats in sight, Dick Dick brought it to a stop. He looked up at the moon, raised his arms skyward and let out a loud, mournful, primitive scream, "Aaahhheeeeeeeeee."

"I've got to think. I've got to think. I've got to think," he yelled aloud to himself. And then he did it again, "Aaaahhheeeeeeeeee," and then he beat his head and face as hard as he could with his fists. "Think, think, think," he screamed.

Dick Dick continued to talk to himself, trying to understand how his perfect master plan had suddenly turned into a fiasco and trying to figure out how to salvage it.

"How the hell could this happen? It was the perfect plan. Somebody someplace screwed up my perfect plan. It was that damn Lenny – he looked at the wrong blueprint. It was that damn Sleepy – he made me sign over everything I own. The two of them are weak. They're wimps. They're pussies. They're afraid of what people will think. They're afraid of what people will say. They're afraid they'll get run out of town. Wimps. Pussies.

"Now they want to jump ship on me. They want to sell the damn land to some farmer for a third of what we paid or sell it for whatever the hell we can get, just to get rid of it.

"I should never have included them in the plan. I should

have done it all by myself. I'm not afraid of what people would think. I don't give a damn what people say. I wouldn't let them run me out of town until I was ready to go. I'd be rich, rich, rich and I could do damned well what I wanted. The hell with them all. I am Dick Dick and I do not have to follow the same rules as other people."

And then, in one magnificent moment, the entire plan presented itself to Dick Dick in one fell swoop. It was perfect. It was three times better than the original plan and it would make him three times richer. It was so damn simple that he was surprised he hadn't seen it from the beginning. He threw back his head and laughed long and loud, sounding like some sinister madman in a horror movie.

He was talking aloud again, outlining his plan step by step. "First, I buy Lenny's and Sleepy's share of the land. They're so spooked and eager to distance themselves from this project that I'll buy their shares for a million each. That puts my total cost for the land at five million. I don't have the money, but I know people who do and I only need to borrow the money for a half day, from Monday morning when I pay Lenny and Sleepy, until Monday noon when Gatlin pays me the twenty million.

"With the fifteen million dollar profit, I'll buy up land for developments, apartment buildings, lumber yards and everything else that will go nuts when construction starts on the prison.

"I'll make hundreds of millions of dollars and when people get mad at me for bringing the prison for the criminally insane to Okoboji, I'll take my hundreds of millions of dollars and move elsewhere and they can deal with it. Screw them. Screw them all!" He was laughing again, like that sinister madman.

"You're one ruthless son-of-a-bitch," a voice said from the back of the boat.

For the third time in less than a day, Dick Dick almost had a heart attack as he whipped around to see who it was, fully expecting to see the barrel of a gun pointing at him.

"Wha, wha what the hell are *you* doing here?" he asked, barely able to get the words out.

"You should check your boat more carefully; you never know what might be lurking in the shadows."

"How long have you been here?" Dick Dick demanded, still not sure if the intruder had a gun. "I thought you were in …"

"Your face is all bloody. Here, dry yourself off," the intruder interrupted.

Dick Dick grabbed the piece of cloth that was flung at him. He looked at it curiously. It was one of the shirts that he and the other Wise Men had printed listing the colleges that Punky had been kicked out of or had flunked out of. They had passed them out to anyone who would agree to wear one and they had thought it was the most hilarious thing they had ever seen.

"Read it," the passenger ordered.

Prior to this moment, Dick Dick hadn't paid any attention to the names on the T-shirts. He only knew that there was quite a list. He began to read aloud, "Yale," "Brown," "Providence," "William and Mar . . . ."

"Providence!" Dick Dick screamed. "Providence – that's in Rhode Island!"

For the second time in fifteen minutes, it all came to him at once, all together, complete, and accurate.

"Aaaahheeeeeeee," he screamed as he ripped the shirt into shreds, throwing strips into the air.

"Damn you, you set me up!" Dick Dick yelled as he lunged at the intruder standing at the back of the boat.

When one person, who isn't actually fat, but who is thick and who has an ass two axe handles wide, lunges at full speed at a smaller, quicker, more maneuverable person, one of two things are apt to happen. One: The thick person will grab the smaller person and easily throw them overboard. Two: The smaller, quicker person will simply sidestep the thick person, who will then be propelled overboard by their own momentum.

Dick Dick made a huge splash as he hit the water, which caused the boat to drift in the opposite direction.

"Help," he yelled, "I can't swim. Help me. I'm going under. Don't do this. Don't do this!"

"How does it feel?" the voice said. *"How Does it feel?"*

Chapter
20

John Smith and "Boots" Booton were out for an early Sunday morning boat ride when they noticed a suspicious-looking unmanned Cobalt bobbing on the water near Terrace Park on the south end of West Lake Okoboji. John used his cell phone to report the boat to the Department of Natural Resources, DNR, who patrols the Iowa Great Lakes.

At almost the same instant, two Okoboji businessmen, who prefer to remain anonymous, were out for a boat ride in the vicinity of Triboji Beach on the north end of the lake. At first they thought that the object floating on the water about a hundred yards off shore was a deflated rubber raft or a plastic bag of garbage. Upon closer inspection, however, they were stunned to find that the object was a man in a grey suit, floating face down. They approached the body quickly but cautiously. They pulled their boat alongside the body and each grabbed a handful of the suit coat and pulled the body up out of the water until the man's face was visible.

"My God!" one of them said as his face turned a whiter

shade of pale, "It's Dick Dick."

They could tell instantly that he had been in the water for quite some time and that he was gone.

They quickly debated, should they pull Dick Dick into the boat or should they leave him in the water so the DNR, and maybe the Sheriff, could inspect the scene for themselves. Ultimately they decided that either way, Dick Dick would still be just as dead and that it would be best to leave the area as undisturbed as possible, until they got some direction from the DNR. A quick call to the DNR confirmed that they had made the right decision.

❖ ❖ ❖

The DNR and the Sheriff's department conducted a three-week investigation into the drowning of Dick Dick, officially ruled it accidental, and closed the case.

The investigation included interviewing all persons known to be friends, business associates, or acquaintances of Dick Dick. Lenny Rosenthal and Stephen "Sleepy" Southworth, III had been with each other at Lenny's home the entire evening and had not seen Dick Dick since the middle of the afternoon when they had assisted him with the sale of LeRoy "Punky" Cox's real estate to a Land Trust.

Punky Cox had spent the entire evening at the Wine Bar celebrating the profitable sale of 960 acres of prime real estate. Around fifteen revelers had spent the entire evening with Punky, enjoying round after round of drinks on Punky and swore that he never left the premises. Oh, he might have wandered down the street to some of the other bars a time or two, but he always came back.

In the two days prior to his death, Dick Dick had spent a considerable amount of time with an out-of-state visitor, Gatlin Guthrie, showing him around the area. Mr. Guthrie had checked out of the Four Seasons Motel around 3 p.m. on Saturday and had checked into a motel in Hutchinson, Kansas at about 11 p.m. that night. The eight hours in between appeared to be a reasonable time to drive that distance.

Dick Dick's three ex-wives were contacted, as a routine part of an investigation into a tragic death.

Each of them said the same thing – if they had been inclined to kill Dick Dick, they would have done it long ago, and two of them said they wished they had. The ex-wives live in Florida, California, and Nevada and each had been with friends or family members on the night of Dick Dick's death.

The DNR and the Sheriff's department discovered several curious factors surrounding Dick Dick's death but were unable to determine their relevance if, in fact, there was any relevance.

Why was Dick Dick boating by himself on a Saturday night wearing a fine suit and necktie?

Why were Dick Dick's head and face bruised and cut? Had he hit his head on the boat and knocked himself out when he went overboard?

There was a gently blowing wind from south to north

Saturday night, so why did Dick Dick's boat end up at the south end of the lake instead of being at the north end where Dick Dick's body was found? This was hotly debated.

Why was the switch turned off on Dick Dick's boat?

How or why did Dick Dick end up in the lake? One possible answer was eliminated when it was found that the zipper to his pants was not unzipped – he had not fallen out of the boat while trying to pee, an activity which claims more than a dozen boaters' lives nationwide every year.

Barb's Detailing had detailed Dick Dick's boat on Saturday morning, polishing every surface of the boat, which would naturally wipe off all fingerprints. However, no fingerprints were even found on the steering wheel – not even Dick Dick's. Why?

When his body was found, Dick Dick was grasping a piece of cloth, about six inches long and an inch wide that appeared to be a fragment of a T-shirt. What was the significance of that, if any?

Perhaps the most curious thing of all was that a seat cushion, that doubles as a floatation device, was found in the water in the vicinity of Dick Dick's body. It was determined that the cushion had come from Dick Dick's boat. Had he grabbed the cushion as he was falling out of the boat and had he clung to the cushion for hours, yelling for help, until he finally wore out and went under? Had he grabbed at the cushion as he hit the water but had it squirted away, out of his reach?

There was one final suspicion, that did not appear in any

official report, but that was widely discussed in the bars and restaurants of Okoboji and that was believed to be a strong possibility by many.

Perhaps someone had thrown Dick Dick overboard and had thrown the flotation cushion into the water, out of his reach, to taunt him and to make it appear to be an accident.

There was no shortage of potential suspects for that deed, since Dick Dick had cheated and lied his way through life and had taken advantage of dozens, if not hundreds, of people along the way. If everyone knew this, why did they deal with him? Well, Dick Dick could be charming and whether they liked him or not, everyone had to admit, he could sell; he could really sell.

Dick Dick had been broke twice and had been rich twice, including being rich, by most people's standards, during the time and events described here. Until the Land Trust purchased Punky's land, that is.

Dick Dick's estate consisted entirely of owning one-third interest in the Okoboji Beneficial Land Trust, which owned 960 acres of fair to poor farm land. Everything else that he had owned had been pledged as security for a loan to buy that land. The other owners of the Land Trust, who were never named, decided to sell the land so Dick Dick's estate could be settled and for reasons of their own that were never revealed. Dick Dick's share of the sale was one million dollars which, coincidentally, was close to the amount that he owed on original loans on his house, Bentley, Cobalt, and other assets.

Dick Dick had been married three times and, predictably, did not leave anything in his will to any of his ex-wives. Dick Dick had no children – a crunching knee from a high-stepping running back in his final college football game had shattered the possibility of ever having children. It was one of the main reasons that Dick Dick's wives left him and was the underlying reason that he continually felt the need to prove himself in business and in sales. To prove to himself that he was, in fact, a man. A real man.

Dick Dick died broke; it's true. If he had lived, though, it would have been only a temporary situation and soon he would have risen from the financial ashes and become richer than he had ever been before. How would he have done it? Through sales, of course. To Dick Dick, sales was a calling of the highest order, and he was, after all, one hell of a salesman.

Epilogue

There. That is my report of the events that occurred in Okoboji in those fateful few days, as I understand them. There are still some unanswered questions and some mysteries surrounding these events, and it appears that they may never be ascertained to everyone's satisfaction.

I suspect that some of you reading this, especially if you are a local who considers yourself to be well-connected with what is going on in Okoboji, will not believe that any of these events could have actually occurred. You are entitled to that belief and clinging to it might make your life more pleasant and less upsetting. It is always unsettling to have to face the possibility that something horrible could occur in a wonderful and magical place like Okoboji.

But, I know the truth. I know what I *believe* to be the truth.

There were many riddles included in my report, some of which were a part of the Great Okoboji Treasure Hunt and others that were shared among friends for fun.

Now, I have a riddle for you and, yes, you do have all of the information that you need to solve this riddle: *Who was in the boat with Dick Dick?*

Peter Davidson